"You actually saw her?"

Lily nodded slowly. "She was crying. And she was afraid."

"Can you see her now?"

Her quick, deep breath sounded like a gasp. "No." She lurched from the chair and stumbled against the coffee table.

McBride's heart jumped to hyperspeed as he hurried to Lily's side. He caught her elbow. "Are you OK?"

Her head lolled forward, her forehead brushing against his shoulder.

He wrapped one arm around her waist to hold her up. Her slim body melted against his, robbing him of thought for a long, pulsing moment. She was as soft as she looked and furnace hot, except for the icy fingers clutching his arm. Her head fell back and she gazed at him, her eyes molten.

Desire coursed through him, sharp and unwelcome.

Available in November 2007 from Mills & Boon® Intrigue

Forbidden Territory
by Paula Graves

Closer Encounters
by Merline Lovelace

Operation: Midnight Guardian
by Linda Castillo

Juliet's Law
by Ruth Wind

Covert Makeover
by Mallory Kane

Dark Revelations
by Lorna Tedder

The Lost Prince
by Cindy Dees

Spin Control
by Kate Donovan

Forbidden Territory
PAULA GRAVES

MILLS & BOON®
Pure reading pleasure

*All the characters in this book have no existence outside the
imagination of the author, and have no relation whatsoever to anyone
bearing the same name or names. They are not even distantly inspired
by any individual known or unknown to the author, and all the
incidents are pure invention.*

*First published in Great Britain 2007
by Harlequin Mills & Boon Limited,
Eton House, 18-24 Paradise Road, Richmond, Surrey TW9 1SR*

© Paula Graves 2006

ISBN: 978 0 263 85761 0

46-1107

*Harlequin Mills & Boon policy is to use papers that are
natural, renewable and recyclable products and made from
wood grown in sustainable forests. The logging and
manufacturing processes conform to the legal environmental
regulations of the country of origin.*

*Printed and bound in Spain
by Litografia Rosés S.A., Barcelona*

This book is dedicated to my mother,
for not laughing when I told her I wanted to
be a writer; to Jenn, for putting up with my
doubts, my fears and my dangling participles;
and to Kris, for believing in this story
when I didn't.

PAULA GRAVES,

Alabama native, wrote her first book, a mystery
starring herself and her neighbourhood friends,
at the age of six. A voracious reader, Paula loves
books that pair tantalising mystery with compelling
romance. When she's not reading or writing, she
works as a creative director for a Birmingham
advertising agency and spends time with her family
and friends. She is a member of Southern Magic
Romance Writers, Heart of Dixie Romance Writers
and Romance Writers of America.

Paula invites readers to visit her website,
www.paulagraves.com.

CAST OF CHARACTERS

Lily Browning – The reluctant psychic's visions of Abby put her in a killer's crosshairs.

J McBride – The jaded cop with a tragic past – he doesn't buy Lily's vision but can't deny she's in danger.

Debra Walters – The ex-wife of Senate candidate Adam Walters is the victim of a deadly car-jacking gone wrong.

Abby Walters – Debra's six-year-old daughter goes missing after her mother's murder.

Adam Walters – Abby's father is in a close race for the US Senate – could his opponent be behind his daughter's kidnapping?

Joe Britt – Adam's campaign manager must keep his distracted candidate focused on the prize.

Gerald Blackledge – The incumbent senator is facing a tougher race than anticipated – how far will he go to win?

Paul Leonardi – Debra Walters's former lover wasn't happy about their breakup – could he be behind the murder/abduction?

Skeet and Gordy – Abby's kidnappers are deadly, but why don't they seem to know what to do with their little victim?

Cal Brody – The FBI agent thinks Lily knows too much not to be involved in Abby's kidnapping.

Rose and Iris Browning – Lily's sisters have special gifts of their own.

Casey – Why is this little girl showing up in Lily's visions of Abby?

Chapter One

The vision came without warning, a door bursting open in her mind.

Frightened blue eyes, red-rimmed from crying.

Freckled cheeks, smudged with tears and dirt.

Red hair, tangled and sweat-darkened.

A terrified cry. "Daddy, help me!"

Lily Browning pressed her fingers against her temples and squeezed her eyes closed. Explosions of light and pain raced through her head like arcs of tracer fire. Around her, a thick gray mist swirled. Moisture beaded on her brow, grew heavy and slid down her cheek.

She opened her eyes, afraid of what she would see.

It was just an empty schoolroom, the remains of the morning's classes scattered about the space—backpacks draped by their straps over the backs of chairs, books lying askew. The kids were still at recess.

"Lily?" A woman's voice broke the silence. Lily jumped.

Carmen Herrera, the assistant principal, stood at the entrance of the classroom, but it was the man behind her who commanded Lily's attention. His dark hair was crisp and close-cut, emphasizing his rough-hewn features and hard hazel eyes. His gaze swept over Lily in a quick but thorough appraisal.

The door in her mind crept open again. She stiffened, forcing it shut, her head pounding from the strain. Pain danced behind her eyes, the familiar opening salvo of a migraine.

"Headache again?" Carmen asked, concerned.

Lily pushed herself upright. "It's not too bad." But already the room began to spin. Swaying, she gripped the edge of the desk.

The man in the charcoal suit pushed past Carmen to cup Lily's elbow, holding her steady. "Are you all right?"

Lily's arm tingled where he touched her. Raw, barely leashed power rolled off him in waves, almost as tangible as the scent of his aftershave. It swamped her, stole her breath.

He said her name, his fingers tightening around her elbow. Something else besides power flooded through her. Something dark and bitter and raw.

She met his gaze—and immediately regretted it.

"Help me, Daddy!" The cry echoed in her head. Fog blurred the edges of her sight.

Swallowing hard, she fought the relentless undertow and pulled her elbow from the man's grasp, resisting the urge to rub away the lingering sensation of his touch. "I'm fine."

"Lily gets migraines," Carmen explained. "Not that often, but when they hit, they're doozies."

Lily heard a thread of anxiety woven in the woman's usually upbeat, calm voice. A chill flowed through her, raising goose bumps on her arms. "Has something happened?"

Something passed between Carmen and the man beside her. "Lily, this is Lieutenant McBride with the police. Lieutenant, this is Lily Browning. She teaches third grade." Carmen closed the classroom door behind her and lowered her voice. "One of our students is missing. Lieutenant McBride's talking to all the teachers to find out whether they've seen her."

Red-rimmed eyes.

Tearstained face.

Frightened cries.

Lily's head spun.

Lieutenant McBride pulled a photo from his coat pocket and held it out to her. She shut her eyes, afraid to look.

"Ms. Browning?" He sounded concerned, even solicitous, but suspicion lurked behind the polite words.

Lily forced herself to look at the picture he held. A smiling face stared up at her from the photo framed by red curls scooped into a topknot and fastened with a green velvet ribbon.

Lily thought she was going to throw up.

"You haven't seen her today, have you?" McBride asked. "Her name is Abby Walters. She's a first-grader here."

"I don't have a lot of contact with first-graders." Lily shook her head, feeling helpless and guilty. The sandwich she'd eaten at lunch threatened to come back up, and she didn't want it to end up on the lieutenant's scuffed Rockports.

"You've *never* seen her?" A dark expression passed across McBride's face. Pain, maybe, or anger. It surged over Lily, rattling her spine and cracking open the door of her mind.

Unwanted sounds and images flooded inside. The lost girl, now smiling, cuddled in a man's arms, listening to his warm voice tell the story of *The Velveteen Rabbit*. Red curls tucked under a bright blue knit cap, cheeks pink with—

Cold. So cold.

Scared.

Screaming.

Crying.

Grimy tears streamed down a face twisted with terror, hot and wet on her cold, cold cheeks. Panic built in Lily's chest. She pushed against the vision, forcing it away.

"We have reason to believe that Abby Walters may have been taken from her mother this morning," he said.

"Where's her mother?"

"She's dead."

The words sent ice racing through Lily's veins. She swallowed hard and lied. "I haven't seen this little girl."

McBride gave her an odd, considering look before he reached into his jacket pocket and pulled out a business card. "If you think of anything that might help us find her, call me."

She took the card from him, his palpable suspicion like a weight bending her spine.

Carmen had kept her distance while McBride talked to Lily, but once he turned back toward the door, she moved past him and took Lily's hand. "Go home and sleep off this headache. I'll send Linda from the office to cover for you." She glanced at the detective, who watched them from the doorway. "I can't believe something like this has happened to one of our kids. I'm working on a migraine myself." She returned to McBride's side to escort him from the room.

Lily thrust the business card into her skirt pocket and slumped against the edge of her desk. Sparks of colored light danced behind her eyes, promising more pain to come. She debated trying to stick out the rest of the afternoon, but her stomach rebelled. She barely made it to the bathroom before her lunch came up.

As soon as Linda arrived to cover her class, Lily headed for the exit, weaving her way through the groups of laughing children returning to their classrooms, until she reached her Buick, parked beneath one of the ancient oak trees that sheltered the schoolyard. She slid behind the wheel and closed the door, gratefully shutting out the shrieks and shouts from the playground.

In the quiet, doubts besieged her. She should have told the detective about her visions. She couldn't make much sense of the things she'd seen, but Lieutenant McBride might. What if her silence cost that little girl her life?

Lily pulled the business card from her pocket and squinted at the small, narrow type made wavy by her throbbing head. The scent of his crisp aftershave lingered on the card. Lily closed her eyes, remembering his square jaw and lean, hard face. And those eyes—clear, intense, hard as flint.

She knew the type well. Give him the facts, give him evidence, but don't give him any psychic crap.

Lieutenant McBride would never believe what she'd seen.

By MIDAFTERNOON, when Andrew Walters called from a southbound jet to demand answers about his missing daughter, McBride realized he faced a worst-case scenario. Less than one percent of children abducted were taken by people outside of their own families. Most child abductions were custody matters, mothers or fathers unhappy with court arrangements taking matters into their own hands.

But there was no custody battle in the Walters case. From all accounts, Andrew Walters had no complaints about the custody arrangement with his ex-wife. Over the phone, at least, he'd seemed genuinely shocked to hear his ex-wife had been murdered.

When he learned Abby was missing, shock turned to panic.

"Did you check her school?" he asked McBride, his voice tight with alarm.

"Yes." The memory of Lily Browning's pale face and wild, honey-colored eyes filled McBride's mind, piquing his curiosity—and suspicion—all over again.

"Is there any reason to think Abby might…" Andrew Walters couldn't finish the question.

"It's too early to think that way."

"Are you sure Abby was with Debra?"

"As sure as we can be." When they'd found Debra Walters dead on the side of Old Cumberland Road, a clear plastic backpack with Abby's classwork folder and a couple of primary readers had been lying next to her. Furthermore, neighbors remembered seeing Abby in the car with Debra that morning when she'd left the house.

Her car, a blue Lexus, was missing.

They'd held out hope that Debra had delivered her daughter to school before the carjacking, but McBride's trip to the school had turned up no sign of Abby.

McBride looked down at his desk blotter, where Abby's photo lay, challenging him. He reached for the bottle of antacid tablets by his pencil holder and popped a couple in his mouth, grimacing at the chalky, fake-orange taste. "We've set up a task force to find your daughter. An Amber Alert has been issued. Her photo will be on every newscast in Alabama this evening. We've set up a phone monitoring system at the hotel where you usually stay when you're in Borland, and a policeman will be within easy reach any time of the day or night. If you get a call from anyone about your daughter, we'll be ready."

"You don't have a suspect yet?" Walters sounded appalled.

"Not yet. There's an APB out on the car, and we've got technicians scouring the crime scene—"

"That could take days! Abby doesn't have days."

McBride passed his hand over his face, wishing he could assure Walters that his daughter would be found, safe and unharmed. But she'd been taken by carjackers who'd left her mother dead. McBride didn't want to think why they'd taken her with them instead of killing her when they'd killed her mother.

In the burning pit of McBride's gut, he knew he'd find Abby Walters dead. Today or tomorrow or months down the road, her little body would turn up in a Dumpster or an abandoned building or at the bottom of a ditch along the highway.

But he couldn't say that to Andrew Walters.

Walters's voice was tinny through the air phone. "Nobody's called in with sightings?"

"Not yet." A few calls had come in as soon as the Amber Alert went out. The usual loons. McBride had sent men to check on them, but, of course, nothing had panned out.

"Come on—when something like this happens, you get calls out your ass." Anger and anxiety battled in Walters's voice. "Don't you dare dismiss them all as crackpots."

"We're following every lead."

"I want my daughter found. Understood?"

"Understood." McBride ignored the imperious tone in Walters's voice. The man was a politician, used to making things happen just because he said so. And God knew, McBride couldn't blame him for wanting his daughter brought home at any cost.

But he knew how these things went. He'd seen it up close and personal. The parent of a lost child was desperate and vulnerable. A nut job with a snappy sales pitch could convince a grieving parent of just about anything.

"We're about to land," Walters said. "I have to hang up."

"One of my men, Theo Baker, will meet you at the airport and drive you to your hotel," McBride said. "I'll be by this evening unless something comes up in the case. Please, try not to worry until we know what it is we have to worry about."

Andrew Walters's bitter laugh was the last thing McBride heard before the man hung up.

McBride slumped in his chair, anger churning in his gut. The world was mostly a terrible place, full of monsters. Killers, rapists, pedophiles, users, abusers— McBride had seen them all, their evil masked by such ordinary faces.

A monster had taken Abby Walters, and the longer he kept her, the less hope they had of ever getting her back alive.

McBride picked up Abby's photo, his expression softening at the sight of her gap-toothed grin. "Where are you, baby?"

She wasn't really a pretty child, all knees, elbows and freckles, but in the picture, the sheer joy of life danced in her bright blue eyes. People would notice a kid like Abby Walters. Even in the photo, she had a way about her.

Her picture had certainly affected Lily Browning, though not how McBride had expected. When he'd shown Abby's picture to others at the school, the grinning child immediately brought smiles to their faces. But Lily had looked ill from the start.

She was keeping secrets.

About Abby Walters? McBride couldn't say for sure, but sixteen years as a cop had honed his suspicious nature to a fine edge. He knew she couldn't have been in on the kidnapping; witness testimony had narrowed down Debra Walters's time of death to sometime between seven-twenty and eight-thirty in the morning. According to Carmen Herrera, Lily Browning had been in a meeting at six-thirty and hadn't left it until seven-forty, when students started trickling in. She'd been in class after that.

But he couldn't forget her odd reaction to Abby's photo.

On a hunch, McBride pulled up the DMV database on his computer and punched in Lily Browning's name. While he waited for the response, he mentally replayed his meeting with her.

He'd noticed her eyes first. Large, more gold than brown, framed by long, dark lashes. Behind those eyes lay mysteries. Of that much, McBride was certain.

She was in her twenties—mid to late, he guessed. With clear, unblemished skin as pale as milk, maybe due to the headache. Or was she naturally that fair? In stark contrast, her hair was almost black, worn shoulder-length and loose, with a natural wave that danced when she moved.

She was beautiful in the way that wild things were beautiful. He got the impression of a woman apart, alone, always on the fringes. Never quite fitting in.

A loner with secrets. Never a good combination.

The file came up finally, and McBride took a look. Lily Browning, no middle initial given. Twenty-nine years old, brown hair, brown eyes—*gold eyes,* he amended mentally. An address on Okmulgee Road, not far from the school. McBride knew the area. Older bungalow-style homes, quiet neighborhood, modest property values. Which told him exactly nothing.

Lily Browning wasn't a suspect. She was just a strange woman with honey-colored eyes whose skin had felt like warm velvet beneath his fingers.

Irritated, he checked the clock. Almost four. Walters's plane would have touched down by now and Baker would be with him, calming his fears. Baker was good at that.

McBride wasn't.

He was a bit of a loner with secrets himself.

As he started to close the computer file, his phone rang again. He stared at it for a moment, dread creeping up on him.

Abby Walters's photo stared up at him from the desk.

He grabbed the receiver. "McBride," he growled.

Silence.

He sensed someone on the other end. "Hello?" he said.

"Detective McBride?" A hesitant voice came over the line, resonating with apprehension. Lily Browning's voice.

"Ms. Browning."

He heard a soft intake of breath, but she didn't speak.

"This *is* Lily Browning, right?" He knew he sounded impatient. He didn't care.

"Yes."

Subconsciously, he'd been waiting for her call. Tamping down growing apprehension, he schooled his voice, kept it low and soothing. "Do you know something about Abby?"

"Not exactly." She sounded reluctant and afraid.

He tightened his grip on the phone. "Then why'd you call?"

"You asked if I'd seen Abby this morning. I said no." A soft sigh whispered over the phone. "That wasn't exactly true."

McBride's muscles bunched as a burst of adrenaline flushed through his system. "You saw her this morning at school?"

"No, not at the school." Her voice faded.

"Then where? Away from school?" Had Ms. Herrera been wrong? Had Lily slipped away from the meeting, after all?

The silence on Lily Browning's end of the line dragged on for several seconds. McBride stifled the urge to throw the phone across the room. "Ms. Browning, where did you see Abby Walters?"

He heard a deep, quivery breath. "In my mind," she said.

McBride slumped in his chair, caught flat-footed by her answer. It wasn't at all what he'd expected.

A witness, sure. A suspect—even better. But a psychic? Bloody hell.

Chapter Two

Heavy silence greeted Lily's answer.

"Are you there?" She clutched the phone, her stomach cramping.

"I'm here." His tight voice rumbled over the phone. "And you should know we don't pay psychics for information."

"Pay?"

"That's why you're calling, isn't it?" His words were clipped and diamond hard. "What's your usual fee, a hundred an hour? Two hundred?"

"I don't have a fee," she responded, horrified.

"So you're in it for the publicity."

"No!" She slammed down the phone, pain blooming like a poisonous flower behind her eyes.

The couch cushion shifted beside her and a furry head bumped against her elbow. Lily dropped one hand to stroke the cat's brown head. "Oh, Delilah, that was a mistake."

The Siamese cat made a soft *prrrupp* sound and butted her head against Lily's chin. Jezebel joined them on the sofa, poking her nose into Lily's ribs. Groaning, she nudged the cats off her lap and staggered to her feet. Half-blinded by the migraine, she made her way down the hall to her bedroom.

The headaches had never been as bad back home in Willow Grove, with her sister Iris always around to brew up a cup of buckbean tea and work her healing magic. But Willow Grove was one hour and a million light-years away.

The phone rang. Lily started to let the answering machine get it when she saw Iris's face float across the blackness of her mind. She fumbled for the phone. "Iris?"

Her sister's warm voice trembled with laughter. "I'm minding my own business, drying some lavender, and suddenly I get an urge to call you. So, Spooky, what do you need?"

The warm affection in her voice brought tears to Lily's eyes. "Buckbean tea and a little TLC."

"Did you have a vision?" Iris's voice held no laughter now.

"A bad one." Lily told her sister about Abby Walters. "The detective on the case thinks I'm a lunatic." She didn't want to examine why that fact bothered her. She was used to being considered crazy. Why should McBride's opinion matter?

"What can I do to help?" Iris asked.

"Does your magic work over the phone?"

Iris laughed. "It's not magic, you know. It's just—"

"A gift. I know." That's what their mother had always called it. Iris's gift. Or Rose's or Lily's.

Lily called hers a curse. Seeing terrified little girls crying for their daddies. Broken bodies at the bottom of a ditch, rain swirling away the last vestiges of their life-blood. Her own father's life snuffed out in a sawmill across town—

"Stop it, Lily." Her sister's voice was low and strangled. "It's too much all at once."

Lily tried to close off her memories, knowing that her sister's empathic gift came with its own pain. "I'm sorry."

Iris took a deep breath. "Do you want me to come there?"

"No, I'm feeling better." Not a complete lie, Lily thought. Her headache had eased a little. Just a little. "Sorry I called you away from your lavender."

Iris laughed. "Sometimes I listen to us talk and understand why people think the Browning sisters are crazy."

Lily laughed through the pain. "I'll visit soon, okay? Meanwhile, don't you or Rose get yourselves run out of town."

Iris's wry laughter buzzed across the line. "Or burned at the stake." She said goodbye and hung up.

Lily lay back against the pillow, her head pounding. Jezebel rubbed her face against Lily's, whiskers tickling her nose. "Oh, Jezzy, today went so wrong." She closed her eyes against the light trickling in through the narrow gap between her bedroom curtains, trying to empty her mind. Sleep would be the best cure for her headache. But sleep meant dreams.

And after a vision, Lily's dreams were always nightmares.

BY FIVE O'CLOCK, the sun sat low in the western sky, casting a rosy glow over the small gray-and-white house across the street from McBride's parked car. He peered through the car window, wishing he were anywhere but here.

When Lily Browning had hung up the phone, his first sensation had been relief. One more wacko off his back. Then he'd remembered Andrew Walters's demand and his own grudging agreement. Call it following every lead, he thought with a grim smile. He exited the vehicle and headed across the street.

Lily Browning's house was graveyard quiet as he walked up the stone pathway. A cool October night was falling, sending a chill up his spine as he peered through the narrow gap in the curtains hanging in the front window.

No movement. No sounds.

He pressed the doorbell and heard a muted buzz from inside.

What are you going to say to her—stay the hell away from Andrew Walters or I'll throw you in jail?

Wouldn't it be nice if he could?

He cocked his ear, listening for her approach. Nothing but silence. As he lifted his hand to the buzzer again, he heard the dead bolt turn. The door opened about six inches to reveal a shadowy interior and Lily Browning's tawny eyes.

"Detective McBride." She slurred the words a bit.

"May I come in? I have some questions."

Her face turned to stone. "I have nothing to tell you."

McBride nudged his way forward. "Humor me."

She moved aside to let him in, late afternoon sun pouring through the open doorway, painting her with soft light. Her eyes narrowed to slits, and she skittered back into the darkened living room, leaving him to close the door.

Inside, murky shadows draped the cozy living room

with darkness. When McBride's eyes finally adjusted to the low light, he saw Lily standing a few feet in front of him, as if to block him from advancing any farther.

"I told you everything I know on the phone," she said.

He shook his head. "Not quite."

Her chest rose and fell in a deep sigh. Finally, she gestured toward the sofa against the wall. "Have a seat."

McBride sat where she indicated. As his eyes adjusted further to the darkened interior, he saw that Lily Browning looked even paler than she had at school earlier that day. She'd scrubbed off what little makeup she'd worn, and pulled her dark hair into a thick ponytail. Despite the cool October afternoon, she wore a sleeveless white T-shirt and soft cotton shorts. She took the chair across from him, knees tucked against her chest, her eyes wary.

Her bare skin shimmered in the fading light. He stifled the urge to see if she felt as soft as she looked.

What the hell was wrong with him? He was long past his twenties, when every nice pair of breasts and long legs had brought his hormones to attention. And Lily Browning, of all people, should be the last woman in the world to make his mouth go dry and his heart speed up.

He forced himself to speak. "How long have you been a teacher at Westview Elementary?"

She answered in a hushed voice. "Six years."

He wondered why she was speaking so softly. The skin on the back of his neck tingled. "Is someone else here?"

Suspicion darkened her eyes. "My accomplices, you mean?"

He answered with one arched eyebrow.

"Just Delilah and Jezebel," she said after a pause.

A quiver tickled the back of his neck again. "What are

they, ghosts? Spirits trapped between here and the after-life?"

A smile flirted with her pale lips. "No, they're my cats. Every witch needs a cat, right?"

"You're Wiccan?"

A frown swallowed her smile. "It was a joke, Lieutenant. I'm pretty ordinary, actually. No séances, no tea leaves, no dancing around the maypole. I don't even throw salt over my left shoulder when I spill it." She pressed her fingertips to her forehead. The lines in her face deepened, and he realized her expression wasn't a frown but a grimace of pain.

"Do you get headaches often?"

Her eyes swept down to her lap, then closed for a moment. "Why are you here? Am I a suspect?"

"You called me, Ms. Browning." He relaxed on the couch, arms outstretched, and rested one ankle on his other knee. "You said you saw Abby Walters—how did you put it? In your mind?"

She clenched her hands, her knuckles turning white.

"Why call me?" he continued. "Do I look like I'd buy into the whole psychic thing?"

"No." Her tortured eyes met his. "You don't. But I don't want to see her hurt anymore."

He didn't believe in visions. Not even a little. But Lily's words made his heart drop. "Hurt?"

"She's afraid. Crying." Lily slumped deeper into the chair. "I don't know if they're physically hurting her, but she's terrified. She wants her daddy."

McBride steeled himself against the sincerity in her voice. "How do you know this?"

Her voice thickened with unshed tears. "I don't know

how to explain it. It's like I have a door in my mind that wants to open. I try to keep it closed because the things behind it always frighten me, but sometimes they're just too strong. That's what happened today. The door opened and there she was."

Acid bubbled in McBride's stomach, a painful reminder of too much coffee and too little lunch. "You actually saw her?"

Lily nodded slowly. "She was crying. Her face was dirty and she was afraid."

"Can you see her now?"

Her quick, deep breath sounded like a gasp. "No."

Tension buzzed down every nerve. "Why not?"

"It doesn't work like that. Please…" She lurched from the chair and stumbled against the coffee table. A pair of cut-glass candlesticks rattled together and toppled as she grabbed the table to steady herself. Out of nowhere, two cats scattered in opposite directions, pale streaks in the darkness.

McBride's heart jumped to hyperspeed as he hurried to Lily's side. He caught her elbow. "Are you okay?"

Her head rose slowly. "Go away."

"You can't even stand up by yourself. Are you drunk?"

"I don't drink." Her head lolled forward, her forehead brushing against his shoulder.

"Drugs?"

He could barely hear her faint reply. "No."

He wrapped one arm around her waist to hold her up. Her slim body melted against his, robbing him of thought for a long, pulsing moment. She was as soft as she looked, and furnace-hot, except for the icy fingers clutching his arm. Her head fell back and she gazed at him, her eyes molten.

Desire coursed through him, sharp and unwelcome.

Ruthlessly suppressing his body's demands, he helped her to the sofa, trying to ignore the warm velvet of her skin beneath his fingers. "What did you take for the headache?"

"I ran out of my prescription." She lay back and covered her eyes with her forearm, as if even the waning afternoon light filtering through the curtains added to her pain.

"I can call it in for you. Do you have any refills left?"

"Just leave me alone."

He should go, and to hell with her. It was probably another con. But she wasn't faking the pain lines etched across her delicate face. "I can call a doctor for you—"

"The prescription bottle's in the drawer by the fridge." Tears slid out from beneath her forearm.

Her weak capitulation gave McBride an uneasy feeling as he headed to the kitchen to find the prescription.

He was back in fifteen minutes, using the keys Lily had given him to let himself back into the house. It was a few minutes after six and night had fallen, cool and blue. He fumbled along the wall for a light switch, but couldn't find one.

Pausing to let his eyes adjust to the dark, he saw the pale sheen of a lampshade a few feet away, outlined in the glow coming through the windows from the streetlight outside. He felt his way to the lamp and turned it on. The muddy yellow circle of light from the low-watt bulb barely penetrated the darkness in the corner where it stood. But it was better than the unrelenting darkness.

Lily lay on the sofa, her arm still over her eyes.

"Ms. Browning?"

She didn't answer.

McBride crossed to the sofa and crouched beside her, watching the slow, steady rise and fall of her chest. She was asleep, without the benefit of the pills he'd just spent more than fifty dollars buying for her.

No matter. She'd probably need them when she woke up.

She shifted in her sleep but didn't awaken. Waiting for her to settle back down, McBride gave in to the male hunger gnawing at his belly and let his gaze wander over her body, taking in the tempting curves and planes. At some point in her sleep, the hem of her T-shirt had slid up, baring a thin patch of smooth, flat belly and the indentation of her navel.

Heat sluiced through him, unexpected and unwanted. Dragging his gaze from that narrow strip of flesh, he pushed himself to his feet and stepped away from her.

He distracted himself with a quick, cop's-eye survey of the living room. Clean. Spare. Simple furniture in neutral tones with just enough color to ward off boredom. He moved closer to the wall to study a framed watercolor, a delicate rendering of a tulip in colors that would be subtle even with full illumination. A neat signature appeared in black appeared in the bottom right corner: Iris Browning. Mother or sister?

Movement to one side caught his eye. A Siamese cat crouched, frozen, near a small iron plant stand, staring at him from between the leaves of a philodendron. McBride barely made out glowing turquoise eyes in a chocolate face.

A shudder ran through him.

Suddenly, a scream split the quiet, snapping the tension

in his spine like a band. Off balance, he stumbled backward into the lamp, knocking it over. The bulb shattered, plunging the room into darkness.

With his heart slamming against his rib cage, he turned to the sofa, peering through the blackness. In the glimmer of light flowing through the window, Lily's face was a pale oval, twisted into a horror mask by her wide-stretched mouth, her scream rising and swelling like a tidal wave, chilling him to the bone.

LILY KNEW IT WAS NIGHT, black as pitch and deathly quiet except for whimpering sobs. She recognized Abby's soft cries.

"Abby?" she whispered.

The child didn't hear her, but stayed where she was, somewhere in the deep blackness, crying in soft little bleats.

Lily knew she was dreaming, that by waking she could spare herself whatever lay beyond the door separating Abby Walters from her abductors. But she couldn't abandon the little girl.

She could almost hear Abby's thoughts, the panicked jumble of memories and fears—Mommy lying on the roadside, blood streaming down her pale hair, tinting the golden strands red.

Mommy, wake up! Am I going to die? Daddy, help me!

Lily heard the rattle of a doorknob and the scraping sound of a dead bolt sliding open. Bright light sliced through the dark room, blinding them both.

Abby screamed.

A whistle shrieked.

Second shift at the lumber mill. Daddy would be home soon.

As she did every afternoon, Lily shut her eyes and watched her father wipe his brow with his worn white handkerchief, then reach for the switch to shut off the large circular saw.

Bam!

A log slipped loose from the hooks and slammed into Daddy's back, pitching him into the spinning steel blade. A mist of red spun off the blade and spattered the sawdust on the table.

Daddy screamed.

Lily awoke in an explosive rush. Smothering blackness surrounded her, her father's scream soaring, deafening her.

Then she realized the scream was her own.

Gentle hands emerged from the blackness, cradling her face. The couch shifted beneath her and a familiar scent surrounded her. Fingers threaded through her hair, drawing her against a solid wall of strength and warmth.

She felt a hammering pulse against her breasts, beating in rhythm with her own racing heart.

A low voice rumbled in her ear. "It's okay."

Her heart stuttered, then lurched back into a gallop as she realized the strong arms wrapped around her belonged to Detective McBride.

Chapter Three

Feeling Lily's warm body stiffen, McBride let her go. "I think you were having a nightmare." He stood and stepped back from the couch. "Do you remember it?"

She hesitated. "No."

"Think you can bear a little light?" McBride turned on the nearest of the two torchiere lamps flanking the couch. Golden light chased shadows to the other side of the room. "Okay?"

"Yes." She met his gaze, her eyes huge and haunted.

He frowned. "You sure?"

"I'm fine. No need to babysit anymore."

Though he had more questions to ask, he decided to let her stew awhile, wondering when he'd come back. "I put your pills on the kitchen counter. It cost fifty-six dollars, but since I broke your light, we'll call it even." He gestured at the lamp lying at a crooked angle, propped up by an armchair. "Sorry."

Her glimmering eyes met his. A pull as powerful as the ocean tide engulfed him, catching him off balance. He forced himself to turn away, move toward the front door.

Sofa springs creaked behind him. He felt her approach,

the hair on the back of his neck tingling. When he turned again, he found her closer than expected. Close enough to touch. He clenched his fists. "Stay away from this case, Ms. Browning. There's nothing in it for you."

"Goodbye, Lieutenant." She opened the front door. Her skin glowed like porcelain in the blue moonlight.

Quelling the urge to touch her, he slipped out the door and hurried to his car. He slid behind the steering wheel and took several deep breaths. When he felt more in control, he dared a quick look at the dark facade of Lily Browning's house.

His lips tightened to a grim line. What the hell was wrong with him? Of all people, he knew better than to let a woman like Lily Browning get under his skin.

He'd learned that lesson the hard way.

SUNLIGHT KNIFED across Lily's bed, waking her. She squinted at the clock on her bedside table. Nine. All that sleep and she still felt as if she'd been run over by a truck.

She pulled her T-shirt over her head, breathing in a faint, tangy scent clinging to the cotton. It took her back to the darkness, to the feel of McBride's strong arms around her. She'd felt safe. Comforted by his solid body against hers, the soothing timbre of his voice in her ear, telling her everything was okay. God, she'd wanted to believe him.

Jezebel jumped from the dresser to the bed and rubbed her furry face against Lily's chin. Lily stroked the Siamese cat's lean body, from silvery mask to long gray tail. "Hungry, Jez?"

After feeding the mewling cats, she retrieved the Saturday morning paper from the front porch. Settling at the kitchen table with a bowl of cereal, she opened the newspaper.

Abby Walters's freckled face stared back at her. Former Wife of U.S. Senate Candidate Found Dead, Daughter Missing, the headline read in bold, black letters.

Abby Walters, age six, had gone missing after her mother was killed in a carjacking Friday morning. The article speculated the attack might be politically motivated. Abby's father and Debra's ex-husband, Andrew Walters, was a state senator running for the U.S. Senate.

The door in her mind opened a crack. Resolutely, she slammed it shut.

"IT WAS A ONE-TIME THING. She threatened to get a restraining order and I quit." The slim, nervous man sitting across the interview table from McBride pushed his wire-rimmed glasses up his long nose with a shaky finger. "My God, y'all don't think I had anything to do with it...."

McBride tapped his pencil on his notepad and let Paul Leonardi stew a moment. The man's dark eyes shifted back and forth as he waited for McBride to speak.

"I was out of town Friday. I left home at five in the morning. You can ask my neighbor—he saw me leave."

McBride pretended to jot a note, but he already knew all about Leonardi's trip to Lake Guntersville for a weekend of fishing and eagle watching. It had taken the task force most of Sunday to track him down after Andrew Walters had fingered Leonardi as the man most likely to leave his ex-wife dead by the side of the road.

"I loved Debra. I'd never hurt her or Abby."

"Lots of men kill the women they love. That's why it's called a crime of passion." McBride felt a glimmer of satisfaction when Leonardi's face went pale at his words. "I did check your alibi. The cabin manager said you didn't show up until noon. That's seven hours to make a two-hour drive to Guntersville. What did you do with the other five hours?"

"God, I don't know! I took the scenic route part of the time. I stopped for gas somewhere around Birmingham, I think. I stopped at an antique store in Blount County and picked up an old butter churn to add to Mom's collection for her birthday coming up. I went by the home store outlet in Boaz to pick up a pedestal sink for the guest bathroom I'm renovating at home." He raked his fingers through his thinning hair. "Damn, I knew I should have waited and done all that on the way back home, but I figured I'd be tired and just blow it off."

McBride wrote down the stops he mentioned, asking for more details. Leonardi couldn't remember the gas station in Birmingham, but he supplied the name of the antique store and the home center outlet. McBride would put a couple of the task force officers on the job of tracking down the man's movements on Friday morning.

"Back to Mrs. Walters for a moment—I understand you showed up at Westview Elementary one afternoon about a month ago, when she was picking up Abby." McBride watched Leonardi carefully as he spoke. The dark-haired man's eyes widened, dilating with alarm. Good. "That's what convinced her to threaten you with a restraining order, wasn't it?"

Leonardi looked down at his hands. "I just wanted to talk to her. I wanted her to tell me why she'd decided to end it."

"She said you were a transition, didn't she? Just a post-divorce ego stroke."

Leonardi blanched. "It was more than that to me."

"But not her. And you couldn't take no for an answer?"

"I didn't think she'd really given us a chance. She has these friends telling her she should go out, have fun, not tie herself down. 'Don't just settle for the first guy who comes along, Debbie. Have some fun, Debbie.'"

"How do you know what her friends said, Mr. Leonardi?" McBride leaned forward. "Did you tap her phones? Did you put a bug in her house? What?"

He pressed his lips tightly together. "I want a lawyer."

"You're not under arrest. Why would you need a lawyer?"

Leonardi's baleful gaze was his only answer.

"When you showed up at the school—how'd you know what time Debra would be picking up Abby? Had you followed her before?"

Leonardi didn't answer.

"Maybe you know somebody who works there," McBride suggested, tapping the folder on the interview table. He flipped it open, exposing an enlarged photocopy of Lily Browning's driver's license photo from the DMV database.

Leonardi's gaze shifted down to the table as McBride intended. His brow furrowed slightly as his gaze skimmed over the photo, but beyond that, he had no reaction.

Not what McBride had been expecting, but he wasn't ready to discount the idea that Lily Browning had a part in Abby Walters's disappearance. "Know what I think, Mr. Leonardi? I think you have a friend who works at the school. She told you when the first grade would be letting out in the afternoon so you'd know exactly when to show up. Did she know about your plans for Friday, too?"

Leonardi's eyes filled with tears. "I didn't kill Debbie. Don't you get it? I lost her, too, just like her friends and her family and her jerk of an ex-husband did. Why aren't you talking to him? Don't you always look at the husband first?"

McBride had already talked to Walters Friday evening, going over his alibi in detail. Over the weekend he'd been able to validate all the times and places Walters had supplied. Of course, it was possible Walters had hired someone to kill his ex-wife, but the autopsy report McBride had found sitting on his desk first thing that morning suggested that Debra Walters's skull fracture might have been accidental, the result of a struggle with the carjackers.

They couldn't even be sure it was anything but a random carjacking. Debra Walters's Lexus hadn't shown up anywhere yet.

Neither had Abby Walters.

McBride's captain had left it up to him to put together a task force for the case. After contacting the FBI and the local sheriff's department to supply their own officers for the team, McBride had picked six of the best cops on the Borland force to assist him.

Sergeant Theo Baker had the job of holding Andrew Walters's hand and keeping him from calling every few minutes for an update. McBride understood the man's anxiety all too well, but he didn't need that distraction.

Some of the task force members were canvassing the area where Debra Walters had died, hoping for witnesses who might have seen something on Friday morning. Some were fielding calls from tipsters, most of them crackpots and attention seekers.

Others were monitoring Friday morning footage from

the handful of traffic cams scattered throughout the city of Borland, hoping they could track Debra's movements from the time she'd left her home to the time she'd stopped on the side of the road to meet her death. McBride didn't hold out much hope for that angle; where she'd died was a lightly traveled back road without any camera surveillance.

"How long do you plan to hold me?" Apparently having a cry put the steel back in Paul Leonardi's spine; he met McBride's questioning look with a steady gaze. "I know my rights. You can only hold me for so long before you either have to charge me or let me go. Unless you think I'm a terrorist or something."

McBride was tempted to toss him in the cages just to make a point, but he quelled the urge. "I'm going to be checking out your alibi, Mr. Leonardi. If everything pans out, no problem. But you shouldn't leave town anytime soon."

"I'm not going anywhere," Leonardi said. "At least, not until after Debbie's funeral. Do you know when it'll be?"

McBride's eyes narrowed as he stood and motioned for Leonardi to follow him out of the interview room. Either the guy was really innocent or he had cojones of titanium. "Check with her ex-husband. He's handling the arrangements."

Back at his desk a few minutes later, McBride grabbed the bottle of antacids on his desk and downed a couple to ease the fire in his gut.

His captain, Alex Vann, chose that moment to pop his head into the office. He eyed the bottle as he sat down across the desk. "You eat too many of those things."

Ignoring the remark, McBride gave him an update on

his interview with Leonardi. "I don't know if he's good for it or not. He has all kinds of motive, but he just doesn't feel right for this thing."

"And the nutso schoolteacher angle?"

McBride arched his eyebrow at the description of Lily Browning. "He didn't really react at the sight of her photo." Nothing beyond the furrowed brow, which could simply mean he was wondering why McBride was flashing Lily Browning's picture.

"Why don't you take a break, McBride? Go get some lunch."

"I'll order something in."

"Not good enough." Vann's jowly face creased with concern.

McBride didn't pretend not to notice. He put down the papers and looked up at his captain. "I'm fine."

"Maybe you should work another case. Take your pick."

"I want this one."

Vann's gaze darkened, but he didn't comment as he walked out of the office.

McBride didn't expect the captain or anyone else to understand. Working the Walters case was like rubbing salt into an open wound, but McBride couldn't let it go. He had to follow it to the bitter end. Find the child. Capture the kidnappers.

See justice done this time.

THE DOOR IN LILY'S MIND flew open without warning, catching her in the middle of grading papers in her classroom while her students played outside at recess. Her pencil dropped from her shaking fingers, rolling to the floor and disappearing in the silvery fog that washed over her in the span of a heartbeat.

Instinct urged her to fight off the battering ram of images, but at the first glimpse of Abby Walters's tear-stained face, her resistance fled. She gave in to the vision's relentless undertow and let it sweep her into the haze.

The mists parted to reveal Abby Walters on the other side, knees tucked to her chin, blue eyes wide and unblinking.

"Abby," Lily breathed.

The misty void deepened. Abby huddled in the looming darkness, covered with something musty-smelling. A blanket? She was trembling. Her teeth chattered.

Lily shivered, goose bumps rising on her arms.

Cold.

She tried to touch the little girl. Her hand felt as if it moved through cold molasses. "Abby, where are you?"

Lily smelled the musty blanket they huddled beneath. She felt vibrations under her, the carpet-covered hump of a drive shaft hard against her left hip. They were in a car.

"They're moving you, aren't they?" Lily felt the tremble beneath her fingers and realized she was finally touching the girl. "Abby, can you feel me here?"

The little girl went still. "Mama?"

Lily felt a surge of excitement. "No, Abby, I'm a friend."

"Help me!" she cried.

"Shut up!" A harsh male voice boomed in front of them.

Lily tried to get her bearings. She and Abby shared the floorboard behind the front passenger seat. The voice had come from there, so someone else was driving. There were at least two kidnappers. Did McBride know that?

Lily put her arms around Abby and concentrated on planting the sensation of touch in the child's mind—skin to skin, warm and soft. Suddenly, the little girl jerked out of her grasp, all contact between them disintegrating into gray mist.

As Lily tumbled into the void, she saw a hand smack Abby's face. The girl whimpered in terror. Lily cried out as the door in her mind slammed shut, cutting her off.

She came back to herself with a jerk. It took a second to reorient herself. She was in her empty classroom. A glance at her watch confirmed that only a few minutes had passed.

A rap on the closed classroom door jangled her nerves. "Lily?" It was Janet, the teacher whose class was next door. The door cracked open and she poked her head in. "Everything okay? I thought I heard a shout."

"Broke a nail," Lily fibbed, forcing a sheepish expression, though her whole body seemed to be vibrating with tension. "Sorry—it was my longest one."

Janet laughed politely, although wariness darkened her eyes. "Just checking." She closed the door again.

Lily buried her face in her hands, unnerved by the close call. She wasn't used to her visions attacking without warning. What if one hit her while class was in session?

She waited for the tightening bands of a migraine, but they didn't come. She should be in agony after such a powerful vision. Why not this time? Because she hadn't had time to fight it off? Was the answer really that simple?

She replayed the vision in her mind, trying to pick up more clues. She'd made contact. Beyond everything else she'd learned, that fact stood out. Never before had she made actual contact with someone in a vision.

But Abby had heard her. Maybe even felt Lily's arms around her. Though she'd been frightened this time, maybe it was possible to make Abby understand Lily wanted to help her. But that meant letting the visions come, whatever they might bring.

Panic bubbled in her gut, tempting her to retreat again, to lock the door in her mind and hide the key forever. Visions were bad things. She'd learned that lesson long ago. She wasn't like Rose, with her happy gift of predicting love matches, which she'd channeled into a successful job as a matchmaker and wedding planner. Nor like Iris, whose gift of empathy helped her ease people's pain and despair.

Lily's gift was darkness, terror, blood and death. She didn't want to explore her visions. She wanted to end them.

But the memory of Abby haunted her. Maybe she could make a difference in this case. If time didn't run out.

She just had to make someone believe her.

As McBride had suspected, Paul Leonardi had caused at least one incident at Westview Elementary, near the beginning of the school year. Unfortunately, if Lily Browning had any connection to Leonardi, neither the principal nor vice principal knew anything about it.

"I doubt it," Carmen Herrera told McBride in her office a little before noon. "Lily's something of a homebody—she doesn't socialize that much, even with other teachers. I doubt she'd have any reason to know Mr. Leonardi."

A loner with secrets, he thought, remembering his earlier assessment of her. Apparently he'd been spot on. "And there was only the one incident?" he asked.

"Yes, just the one. It wasn't really that big a deal—he didn't resist when security asked him to leave. I didn't get the feeling he was really dangerous. Just heartbroken." Carmen flashed a rueful smile. "We've all been there once or twice, haven't we?"

He thanked her for her time and headed for the exit, slowing as he reached the half-open door to Lily Browning's classroom. Today, it was full of children, who sat with rapt attention as they listened to Lily reading.

He wasn't familiar with the book she'd chosen, but as she told the rollicking tale of a girl and her pet cat braving a violent thunderstorm to reach the girl's injured father, he found himself seduced by her musical voice.

He paused outside the doorway to get a better look at her. She was perched on the edge of her desk, legs dangling. Today she wore her hair up in a coil, with wavy tendrils curling around her cheeks and neck.

It was soft, he remembered. Sweet-smelling, like green apples. He could still recall how she felt in his arms, trembling from her nightmare.

"That's it for today, ladies and gentlemen," Lily announced as she reached a shocking cliffhanger at the end of the chapter. She closed the book, came around the desk and slid it into her top drawer. Scattered groans erupted.

"Aw, Ms. Browning!"

"Can't we read one more chapter?"

"If we finish the book today, what will we have to read tomorrow?" Laughter tinging her voice, she rose from her desk and started passing out sheets of paper. "Besides, Mrs. Marconi is waiting for you in the library. Let's go, single file."

McBride's lips curved. Years passed, things changed, but teachers still lined their students up single file. He backed away, hoping to make a quick exit without being caught eavesdropping, but he hadn't made it down the hall more than a couple of steps when Lily's voice called out to him.

"Lieutenant McBride?"

Busted.

Chapter Four

Anxiety rippled through Lily's belly. Why was Lieutenant McBride here? Had something happened? "Is there news?"

The single file line of students flowing out the door behind her began to devolve into chaos. Tamping down her fear, she quickly brought them back into order, glancing over her shoulder to make sure McBride hadn't left while she was distracted. "Please wait here—I'll be back in just a minute."

She headed up the hallway with her brood, quelling small mutinies with a firm word or a quick touch of her hand on a troublemaker's shoulder. Once they were out the door in the custody of the librarian, she hurried back to her classroom, afraid McBride would be gone. But she found him sitting on the edge of her desk, his expression unreadable.

"Is there news about Abby?" she asked.

"No. I was just following another lead."

She cocked her head to one side. "Here?"

"Ever met a man named Paul Leonardi?" His gaze focused like a laser on her face.

She frowned, searching her memory. "Not that I remember."

"He had to be escorted from the school grounds a couple of months ago, near the start of the school year."

"Oh, that guy." It had caused a big stink, generating a dozen new security policies. "Yeah, I heard about it, but I didn't see it happen."

He pulled a piece of paper from his pocket. "You never saw this guy?"

She glanced at the paper. It looked like a driver's license photo. The man in the picture was nice-looking in an ordinary sort of way. She shook her head. "Do you think he's one of the kidnappers?"

"One of them? You think there's more than one?" McBride's eyes changed color, from smoky brown to mossy green. "Why do you think there's more than one kidnapper?"

She licked her lips. "I had another vision. Abby in a car, huddled under some sort of blanket. One of the kidnappers hit her." McBride's hard gaze made Lily want to crawl into a hole, but she pushed ahead. "Whoever struck Abby was in the passenger seat, so someone else had to be driving."

He rose from the edge of her desk. "If you remember anything about Mr. Leonardi, let me know."

She caught his arm. "I can help you if you'd let me."

He looked down at her hand, contempt in his eyes. "I'm up to my eyeballs in help, Ms. Browning. Every crackpot in the state seems to know what happened to Abby Walters."

She dropped her hand quickly. "Including me?"

"Some of my people are handling the crackpot calls. I'll tell them to expect yours." He headed out to the hall.

Torn between irritation and humiliation, Lily watched him reach the exit and step outside. He couldn't have made it any clearer that he didn't want to hear what she had to say.

She'd have to deal with her visions of Abby her own way.

LILY HATED FUNERAL HOMES.

The newspaper had listed the time and place for the pre-funeral viewing. Her stomach churned at the thought of crashing the wake, but if she was going to find Abby, she needed to start with the people closest to her. Her father. Family and friends. Proximity to people who knew the subjects had always made her visions stronger in the past. It was one reason Lily had become something of a recluse in her personal life. Avoiding people was self-defense.

But this time, she needed the visions to come.

She spotted Carmen Herrera getting out of her car. Lily stepped out of her own car and met the assistant principal halfway to the door. "I was afraid I'd missed you."

Carmen smiled sadly, putting her hand on Lily's arm. "Thanks for volunteering to come with me. I hate wakes."

"Me, too." She followed Carmen up the steps to the funeral home entrance, distracted by a spattering of camera flashes.

"The press." Carmen grimaced. "Ghouls."

More flashes went off as they entered. The foyer's faux marble floors and gilt furnishings gave the room a cold, austere feeling. *Funereal,* Lily thought with a bubble of dark humor. She tamped down a nervous giggle.

The small viewing chapel was packed with a combination of mourners and a few people Lily suspected were reporters who'd hidden their agendas along with their notepads to get inside.

Not that Lily could quibble about hidden agendas.

She signed the guest book and went with Carmen to the front, forcing herself to look at the body in the coffin.

Had Debra Walters been as lovely in life as the powdered, waxed and beautifully coiffed body in the casket? Seeing her now, Lily realized she did look a bit familiar. Maybe Mrs. Walters had been at a parent-teacher event earlier in the year. Or maybe it was just the resemblance between mother and daughter that struck a chord.

"There's Mr. Walters." Carmen moved toward a well-dressed man surrounded by a handful of fellow mourners. His newspaper photo didn't do justice to his lean good looks, Lily thought.

She should join Carmen, take advantage of the opening to meet Abby's father and see if he'd be receptive to her unusual method of finding his daughter. But a combination of guilt and fear held her back. There was something unseemly about using these particular circumstances to approach him with her offer of help.

"They did a good job, didn't they?" a man's voice asked.

Lily jerked her attention toward the questioner, a familiar-looking man of medium height with dark hair and mournful brown eyes. He met her gaze briefly before looking back at the body.

"But they didn't capture who she really was." Sadness tinged his voice. "She was the most alive person I ever knew."

This was the man in the picture McBride had showed her, Lily realized. The one who'd come to the school looking for Debra. The hair on her arms prickled.

"Paul Leonardi. Debra and I dated a few months ago." He held out his hand. "You look familiar. Do I know you?"

"No." She made herself shake his hand. It was damp and hot, his handshake limp. She quelled the urge to wipe her palm on her skirt. "I'm Lily. I teach at Abby's school."

His expression darkened. "Horrible about the little girl."

Interesting, she thought. He'd said "the little girl" as if Abby were an afterthought.

Paul's eyes shifted away from her, his brow creasing. "Great. The cops are here."

Lily followed his gaze and met the narrowed eyes of Lieutenant McBride. She looked away quickly, her heart clenching. Of course he was here. She should have anticipated it. He'd be hoping for the killer to show up.

Paul gritted his teeth. "Can't I have one night to mourn her without the Gestapo breathing down my neck?"

"He has a job to do," Lily responded, surprised to be defending McBride. "Don't you want him to catch Debra's killer?"

"Of course." Paul directed his glare her way.

Unless you're the killer, she thought, her heart leaping into her throat. Obviously, he'd had feelings for Debra, and from the way he'd phrased things earlier Lily gathered the relationship had ended, probably before he was ready.

Not a bad motive for murder.

To her relief, Carmen Herrera approached, Andrew Walters a step behind her. She put her hand on Lily's shoulder. "Lily, this is Mr. Walters, Abby's father. Mr. Walters, Lily Browning."

To Lily's left, Paul Leonardi stepped away before she

was forced to make an introduction. He blended back into the rest of the crowd.

"It was kind of you and Mrs. Herrera to come. Abby's teacher was here earlier to pay her respects, but it means a lot that you both came as well." Andrew Walters took Lily's hand, his expression eager. "Do you know my daughter well, Ms. Browning?"

Lily glanced at Carmen before she answered Walters's question. "I don't know her, really, but from all accounts she's a delightful child."

"She is." Andrew Walters's gaze softened.

Carmen put her hand on Lily's shoulder. "I'll be back in a sec. I see someone I should say hello to." She drifted away, leaving Lily alone with Andrew Walters.

"I hope you find Abby soon," she told him.

His expression hardened with determination. "I'll do whatever it takes to get her back."

She almost told him what she knew then and there. But the sight of McBride bearing down on them held her in check.

"Mr. Walters?" McBride's voice rose over the soft murmurs of conversation surrounding them. He stepped forward, taking Andrew Walters by the elbow and drawing him away. "I need to speak to you."

Carmen crossed to Lily's side. "Ready to go?"

"Yes."

"Is that Lieutenant McBride talking to Mr. Walters?" Carmen asked as they headed for the exit.

"Maybe," Lily replied, keeping to herself the fact that Lieutenant McBride's rough-hewn features and hard hazel eyes were indelibly imprinted in her memory.

"STILL NOTHING FROM the task force?" His voice laced with desperation, Andrew Walters shifted from one foot to the other.

McBride forced himself to look away from Lily Browning's retreating figure. "We're still following leads."

"Is Ms. Browning one of those leads?" Walters asked. When McBride remained silent, he added, "You seemed eager to get me away from her just now."

McBride took a deep breath through his nose. He should have known a politician would be perceptive. And since Lily Browning proved by coming to this wake that she wasn't going to back off, it was a good idea to inoculate Walters with the truth before she made her next attempt to contact him. "I wanted you away from her because Ms. Browning believes she's having visions of Abby."

Walters cocked his head to one side. "Visions?"

"Obviously she's a crank."

"But what if—"

The hopeful gleam in Walters's eyes made McBride cringe. "Don't do this, Mr. Walters. You want to believe she can help you. I get that. I do. You need somebody to tell you Abby's okay and she's coming back to you any day now. Ms. Browning will tell you she can lead you to her." Acid spewed into McBride's stomach. "But she can't. She doesn't know anything."

"And you do?" Walters's cold voice seemed to grate on McBride's spine. "*You* think Abby's dead, don't you?"

McBride couldn't deny it, so he said nothing.

"I don't believe that, Lieutenant." Walters lifted his chin. "And if Lily Browning thinks she can help me find my daughter, I want to hear what she has to say."

"There have to be better leads to follow. What about a political angle? Is that possible?"

Walters's look of resolve faltered. "Maybe. I have a very powerful opponent with powerful backers. I don't know what they're capable of."

"We're looking at Blackledge, I assure you." The savvy old senator was barely leading Walters in the latest polls. Probably because of his divorced status, Walters had made his relationship with his daughter the focal point of his campaign ads, stressing family values in an attempt to assure the conservative local voters he was a solid citizen they could trust in Washington.

Maybe Blackledge or one of his people had figured taking the daughter would ensure Walters dropped out of the race. After all, the doting father could hardly keep up the campaign while his kid was missing. A thin motive, but not out of the realm of possibility, especially where politics were involved.

Of course, the same could be said of Andrew Walters.

However, Walters had an alibi. And McBride couldn't see a motive for killing his ex-wife and getting rid of his daughter. Everyone McBride had talked to agreed that Walters and his ex had remained friends after the divorce. Walters never missed a child support payment, supplying more than the court-agreed amount.

He might have means, but he lacked motive and opportunity. And Walters couldn't possibly be faking the panic underlying every word he spoke.

"Mr. Walters, I know what you're feeling—"

The state senator narrowed his eyes. "I doubt it. Now, if you'll excuse me, I have other people to talk to."

Torn between sympathy and anger, McBride watched

Walters leave. He hadn't been feeding him a line. He knew exactly what the man was going through.

Every excruciating moment of it.

McBride gravitated to the open casket and gazed down at Debra Walters. She was lovely in death, her pretty features composed and calm, as if she were merely asleep. Thick makeup designed to make the dead look better than the living covered the bruise on her temple.

McBride's stomach roiled. Laura's casket had been closed.

"How can you be working on a case like this?" Theo Baker joined McBride at the casket, his dark eyes full of concern.

McBride's stomach burned. "Abby's father has to know what happened to her." Even if she was dead. It was not knowing that killed you.

An inch at a time.

DEBRA WALTERS'S FUNERAL was a brief, solemn affair, held at graveside. A smattering of people sat in metal folding chairs under a white tent that shielded the casket from the bright October sunlight. Several more filled out the circle of mourners around the site, including dozens of cameramen from local stations and national networks. Another clump of people gathered around a tall, silver-haired man Lily recognized as Senator Gerald Blackledge.

Strange, his being here. Or maybe not—the senator's opponent had just lost his ex-wife to foul play. Maybe Blackledge thought if he didn't appear for the funeral, he'd look as if he had something to hide.

And a public show of compassion couldn't hurt, she supposed.

Andrew Walters gave a brief, eloquent eulogy, captured for posterity by the news cameras. Ever the politician, he managed to come across both sad and commanding, an achievement Lily couldn't help but admire, though she found his self-control almost as discomfiting as Gerald Blackledge's decision to attend the funeral and turn it into a media circus.

But maybe politicians had no choice but to be "on" all the time, with so many cameras around, waiting for them to stumble.

A cadre of reporters hovered about, talking into microphones in hushed tones that might have been unobtrusive if there weren't a dozen other newspeople doing the same thing at the same time. Across from Lily, on the other side of the circle of mourners, stood Lieutenant McBride, his eyes hidden by mirrored sunglasses.

But she felt the full weight of his disapproval.

Too bad. She'd given him a chance to help Abby. Now she was handling things her own way.

She didn't have to approach Andrew Walters after the service; he sought her out almost as soon as the preacher finished his prayer and the casket was lowered into the ground.

"I spoke to Lieutenant McBride this morning." He kept his voice low, taking her elbow and guiding her away from the crowd. "He says you claim you had a vision of Abby. Is that true?"

Unprepared for his straightforward question, she stumbled, grabbing Andrew's arm to steady herself. A murmur went up among the reporters and they shifted toward them. Lily quickly let go of Andrew's arm. "Yes, it's true, but we can't talk about it here."

"Come by my hotel room tomorrow evening. We'll discuss it then," Andrew murmured, before carefully stepping away.

Turning, Lily came up against a wall of black-clad men with earpieces. Bodyguards, she realized as the men parted like the Red Sea and Senator Gerald Blackledge strode through the gap, hand outstretched.

"Andrew, I'm so sorry to hear about your ex-wife and daughter. If I can do anything to help, you mustn't hesitate to use me. Understand? Politics has no place in this situation."

The irony of the senator's words, juxtaposed against the flash of camera bulbs and the sea of camcorders and microphones, forced a bubble of nervous laughter up Lily's throat. She swallowed it, looking for her chance to slip away. But before she moved a step, Blackledge caught her elbow.

"Please, don't go on my account, Miss…?"

Andrew's mouth tightened. "Lily Browning, this is Senator Gerald Blackledge. Senator, this is Lily Browning. She teaches at the school my daughter attends."

The senator enveloped her hand in a firm handshake. "A delight to meet you, Ms. Browning. My mother taught English for thirty years." He looked sincerely interested, but Lily imagined a man who'd been a senator for twenty years had probably honed his acting ability to perfection.

"Really?" Lily responded politely, catching a glimpse of McBride a few feet away. Unnerved by his scrutiny, she murmured an excuse and moved aside, trying to avoid the cameras ringing them. She'd almost made it to the parking area when someone grabbed her arm. Whirling, she came face-to-face with McBride.

He'd removed his sunglasses, exposing her to the full brunt of his fury. "Don't do this, Ms. Browning."

She jerked her arm from his grasp. "Did I break a law?"

He didn't answer.

"I didn't think so." She headed toward her car.

McBride fell into step, his long strides easily matching hers. "He's vulnerable and desperate. The last thing he needs is someone promising she can bring his baby back home to him when we both know damn well you can't."

She unlocked her car and opened the driver's door, putting its solid bulk between her and McBride. "I know you don't think she's still alive."

His only visible reaction was a tightening of his lips.

"But I know she is, and I'm not going to wait around for you to get over your knee-jerk skepticism before I do something about it."

She started to get into the vehicle, but he grabbed the door before she could pull it shut behind her. Looking down at her over the top, he narrowed his eyes. "If you really know Abby's alive, answer me this—why have four days passed without anyone calling with a ransom demand?"

Lily's stomach knotted. She had no explanation for that.

"Think about it." He let go of the door and stepped away.

HE WATCHED FROM THE gravesite, his heart pounding. Who was this woman with the knowing eyes? What could she know about what had happened to Abby?

He'd planned so carefully. Worked out all the details, figured the odds. He'd visualized just what would happen, down to the lightly traveled shortcut Debra took every weekday morning on her way to Abby's school. He knew where to stage the surprise attack, and how quickly Debbie would be scared into compliance.

It was supposed to be fast. Grab the girl and go, leaving Debra to sound the alarm and put the rest of the plan in motion.

But she had fought back.

He hadn't thought she'd fight back. She'd always been such a marshmallow.

Everything had gone terribly wrong. And now there was Lily Browning, with her strange gold eyes and her knowing look, claiming she'd seen a vision of Abby.

His heart twisted with growing panic.

What if she really had?

A PHOTO OF LILY, Andrew Walters and Gerald Blackledge made the front page of Wednesday's *Borland Courier*. The teacher's lounge was abuzz when she arrived at school that morning.

"At least it's a good picture. And they spelled your name correctly," Carmen Herrera pointed out when Lily groaned at the sight of her face above the fold.

"I didn't give anyone my name." There was no mention of her in the body text, at least. "I guess Mr. Walters told them."

"Or the senator," Carmen suggested.

That was also possible—a jab at Mr. Family Values, consorting with a new woman right there at his ex-wife's funeral. What would voters think?

Worse, what would Lieutenant McBride think when he got a look at her name and face plastered across the front page?

She half expected to find him waiting on her doorstep when she arrived home that afternoon, storm clouds gathering in his eyes, so she was almost disappointed to find no one waiting. But when she entered her house to find her phone ringing, she wasn't surprised. She was listed in the directory; any reporter with a taste for a trumped-up scandal could look her up.

Lily grabbed the phone and took a deep breath, steeling herself for unpleasantness. "Hello?"

"Lily Browning?"

She knew that voice. The kidnapper's harsh drawl was unmistakable. Lily's heart slammed into her ribs. "You have Abby Walters."

There was a long pause over the phone. When the man spoke, he sounded wary. "How'd you know that?"

"Is she okay?" Lily's mind raced, wondering what to do next. Nobody was expecting the kidnappers to call here; all the recording equipment was no doubt set up at Andrew Walters's hotel, waiting for a ransom demand. As she scrabbled for something to write with, her gaze fell on the answering machine attached to her phone.

The kind that allowed her to record incoming conversations.

She jabbed the record button with a shaking finger.

"She's fine, for now," the kidnapper said.

"You hit her, you son of a bitch!"

There was a brief silence on the other end before the man spoke in a hushed tone. "What the hell are you?"

Lily ignored the question. "Let me talk to her."

"Don't be stupid."

Shivers raced up her spine, followed by the first hint of gray mist clouding the edges of her vision. Gripping the phone harder, she fought off the sensation. "Why are you calling me instead of Mr. Walters?"

"You think we don't know the cops have his phone tapped? We've been looking for a way to contact him away from his hotel." The caller laughed. "Then we seen your picture in the paper. Lucky break, ain't it?"

Lily sank down on the floor, tucking her knees close to her body. "You want me to pass along your demands to Mr. Walters?"

"Tell him it's time to pay up. We'll be in touch."

She heard a soft clicking noise. "Wait!"

But the man had already disconnected.

She slammed down the phone and covered her face with shaking hands. The door in her mind bulged, trying to force its way open, but she continued to fight the vision.

She had to call McBride.

With pain lancing behind her eyes, she checked the tape in the answering machine, terrified she'd pushed a wrong button and failed to record the kidnapper's message. But the harsh drawl was there. "Tell him it's time to pay up."

She shut off the recorder and dialed McBride's cell phone number. He answered on the second ring. "McBride."

She released a pent-up breath. "It's Lily Browning. The kidnappers just phoned me."

"What?" He sounded wary.

She told him about the call. "I managed to record most of it on my answering machine. Do you want me to play it for you?"

"No, I'm on my way." He hung up without saying goodbye.

By the time he arrived ten minutes later, her head was pounding with pain, the vision clawing at her brain. She didn't bother with a greeting, just flung the door open and groped her way back to the sofa, concentrating on surviving the onslaught of pain in her head. She wished she could escape to her room and let the vision come, but she had to stay focused.

McBride went straight to the answering machine. "What time did the call come in?"

She altered her expression, trying to hide the pain. "The phone was ringing when I got home—maybe three-forty?"

He listened to the tape twice before he pulled it from the machine. "I'll get this to the feds on the task force, see if they can clean it up a little, pick up some background noises. Maybe we can pinpoint where he was calling from. And I'll take a copy to Mr. Walters, see if he recognizes the voice."

"I recognized it," she said, keeping her voice low out of self-defense as the pounding in her skull grew excruciating. She tried to say *something* more, but the merciless grip of the impending vision tightened. Helpless against it, she sank into a whirlwind of dark, cold mist.

Chapter Five

The mist parted to reveal a small, blue-clad figure. Lily's heart quickened at the sight of dirty red curls. "Abby?"

The child didn't respond.

The mist dissipated, revealing a tiny room with mottled faux oak paneling and faded yellow curtains splotched with sunflowers. A tiny bed occupied the entire wall under the metal-frame window. A prefab house, or maybe a mobile home.

"Abby?" she whispered again.

The child sat on the cot, huddling in a ball against the wall, tears sparkling on her grimy cheeks. With horror, Lily realized one of the smudges there was a bruise.

Abby stirred, her blue eyes darting around the room.

"Abby, it's me. Lily. I talked to you the other day. Remember? In the car?"

The little girl's eyes widened. Her pink rosebud mouth opened, making words without sound. But Lily heard her thoughts, as clearly as if the child had spoken. "Are you a ghost?"

"No, I'm not. I'm not scary at all." Lily touched her. "Can you feel that?"

"Yes." Abby whispered back in her mind.

"Good. See, I'm not hurting you, am I?"

Abby shook her head.

"My name is Lily. I teach at your school. Maybe you remember me from there?"

"I can't see you," Abby replied.

Lily wondered if she could make herself visible to Abby. Was it even possible? She concentrated on seeing herself in the vision. She looked down at Abby's arm and visualized her own hand gently squeezing the soft flesh. But nothing happened.

Abby's eyes welled up. "I can't see you!" she whimpered.

Aloud.

"Shh, baby, don't say it out loud." Lily held her breath, fearing the arrival of Abby's captors. After a few seconds passed and no one came, she exhaled. "Remember, Abby, you have to *think* everything. We don't want the mean men to hear you."

"Why can't I see you?" Abby's thoughts were a frantic whisper. "Where are you?"

"I'm at my house, but I'm thinking real hard about you, and my mind is touching your mind." Lily didn't know how to make Abby understand. She didn't really understand it herself.

"Like a psychic?" Abby asked. "Like on TV?"

Close enough, Lily thought. "Yes."

"Can you tell my future?"

"I know you're going to be okay. I'm going to help you."

"I want to go home." Abby started to cry. Lily put her arms around her, surprised by the strength of the mental connection. She felt the child's body shaking against hers, heard the soft snuffling sound. Warm, wet tears trickled down Lily's neck where the little girl's face lay.

"Soon, baby—" Lily stopped short.

Something began to form at the edge of her vision.

Her eyes shifted to the emerging image, her grip on Abby loosening. She drew her attention back to Abby, but not before she saw a shape begin to take form in the mists.

Another little girl.

"Lily? Where are you?" Abby jerked away, her body going rigid. "They're coming!"

Suddenly she was gone, and Lily was alone in the fog.

But not completely alone.

In the distance, she still saw the hazy shape of the unknown little girl. But as she approached the child, the image shimmered and faded into gray.

The mists began to clear, and Lily found herself in her living room, slumped on the sofa. The afternoon sunlight had begun to wane, shadows swallowing most of the room. Maybe ten minutes had passed since the vision started.

Real time. I was really there.

But who was the other little girl?

"Ms. Browning?" The sound of Lieutenant McBride's voice made her jump.

He sat on her coffee table, his expression shuttered. He'd shed his jacket and rolled up the sleeves of his white dress shirt to his forearms. "Back among the living?" he asked dryly.

Her head pounded from the fight she'd put up to hold off the vision until she could tell McBride about the call. Staggering to her feet, she headed to the kitchen for her pills.

The detective followed. "Another headache?"

She swallowed a pill and washed it down with water from the tap. "If you're just going to mock me for the rest of the afternoon, go away. Don't you have a tape to analyze?"

"The feds are on the way to pick it up. They'll give Sergeant Baker in my office a copy to take over to Mr. Walters."

At least Mr. Walters would know why she didn't make their meeting tonight, she thought.

McBride sat down at her kitchen table and waved toward the chair next to him. "I'm all yours for the evening. So why don't you tell me what the hell just happened in there?"

"I need to lie down."

His eyes narrowed. "Fine. I'm not going anywhere."

She ignored the threat and staggered to her room, wincing as sunlight sliced through the parted curtains, shooting agony through her skull. Too ill to draw the blinds, she groped her way to her bed and lay down, covering her eyes with her forearm.

She heard quiet footsteps approaching on the hardwood floor. She could feel McBride's gaze on her. "You okay?"

"I just need to sleep."

"Do the headaches usually come when you have visions?"

"Only when I fight them," she murmured through gritted teeth.

"Why would you fight them?"

Couldn't he just leave her alone? "They scare me. I don't usually like what I see."

His footsteps sounded again, this time accompanied by the sound of drawing drapes. The thoughtfulness of the action surprised her.

His expression was hard to read in the darkness, but she thought she detected a hint of gentleness in his craggy features. "Thank you," she murmured.

His expression hardened. "Don't thank me yet."

He turned and left her alone in the dark.

"THE FEDS WILL BE bringing you a copy of the tape," McBride told Theo Baker over the phone. "Get it to Andrew Walters ASAP." Maybe Walters would recognize the voice.

And maybe pigs would fly.

McBride hung up and slumped on the sofa, tension banding across his shoulders. His gut churned like a whirlpool, but his antacids were at the office.

How convenient that a day after he'd mentioned the fact that the kidnappers hadn't yet called, Lily Browning should be the one contacted. Surely she saw how guilty it made her look. Yet she'd phoned him instead of Andrew Walters, who'd be far less skeptical about her motives.

What kind of game was she playing? And why had the caller sounded so spooked when she'd accused him of hitting Abby? "What the hell are you?" he'd asked. Either the guy was a heck of an actor or he didn't know Lily or what she claimed to be.

There could be an explanation for that, of course. Maybe the kidnappers were hired thugs, and Lily's connection was to whoever had hired them to grab the girl. Paul Leonardi? McBride had watched Leonardi closely at the funeral home. When he'd approached Lily, it had seemed like a first-time meeting.

Gerald Blackledge? He'd made a point to talk to Lily at the funeral. And what kind of man would commandeer a solemn occasion to score political points? A man who thought abducting a little girl would drive her father out of the senatorial race?

McBride's belly burned like fire.

WHEN LILY WOKE, the clock on her dresser read 7:45 p.m. Around her, all was so quiet she wondered if McBride had given up and gone for the night. But when she padded barefoot to the kitchen, she found him sitting in one of the chairs facing the counter, where Jezebel perched like a stone statue, her blue eyes crossed in a baleful glare.

"I don't think she'd want you on the counter," McBride was telling the cat. "In fact, why don't you come over here and see me?"

Jezebel's eyes narrowed, but she didn't budge.

"Come on, kitty. Come see McBride. Come on," he crooned.

Lily bit back a chuckle of sympathy as Jezebel turned and started grooming herself.

McBride's voice dropped to a sexy rumble. "Got a big ol' lap here, puss. And I've been told I have talented hands. You don't know what you're missing."

A quiver rippled down Lily's spine.

"Oh, I see, you like playin' hard to get. You must be a female." McBride sat back and propped one ankle on the opposite knee. "That's okay. I'm a patient man. I can wear you down."

Lily decided to end the standoff before his sexy drawl melted her into a puddle in the kitchen doorway. "You're trying to seduce the wrong woman."

The detective's head whipped around in surprise.

"Jezzy hates everyone but me. It drives my sister Rose crazy." Lily picked up the cat and cuddled her a moment, smiling at his flummoxed expression when Jezebel melted in her arms, butting her face against Lily's chin.

She set her on the floor. "Delilah's the pushover."

As if Lily had spoken a command, Delilah entered the kitchen, tail twitching, and wound herself around McBride's ankle. He reached down and scratched the cat's ears. Delilah rewarded him with a rumbling purr of pleasure.

"Better?" Lily sat across from him, glancing at the loose sheets of notepaper littering her kitchen table.

He gave her a considering look, gathering up the papers. His short hair was mussed and spiky, softening the hard lines of his face. His presence filled her kitchen, branding every inch of space he occupied as his own.

And a traitorous part of her liked the idea that he belonged here. With her.

The corded muscles of his forearms rippled as he stacked the sheets in a neat pile in front of him. When he spoke, his voice was gruff. "Headache better?"

"Yeah." Awareness shuddered through her, a magnet drawing her toward him. She'd already leaned his way when she caught herself. She rose from the table, wishing she hadn't closed the distance between them. "Have you eaten dinner?"

"No. Didn't realize what time it was."

She pulled sliced turkey, cheese and a jar of mayonnaise from the refrigerator. "I can make you a sandwich."

The legs of his chair scraped against the tile floor. She felt his body heat flow over her a second before he put his hand on her shoulder. "Sit down. I'll fix it."

She turned toward him, caught off guard when he didn't step back. Her gaze settled on the full lower lip that kept his mouth from looking unapproachably stern. His square jaw was dark with a day's growth of beard. If he bent his head now and touched his cheek to hers, how would it feel?

Her legs shook as if she'd run for miles, and her skin felt itchy and tight. She wished she could blame her shivers on the events of the afternoon, but she knew better.

Unlike Jezebel, she was beginning to find McBride nearly irresistible. Much to her alarm.

His grip on her shoulder loosened, though he didn't drop his hand away. His thumb brushed across her clavicle, sending tremors pulsing along her nerves. The moment stretched taut, the tension between them exquisite. Her breath caught in her throat, her lips trembling in anticipation of the moment when he'd finally bend his head and end the torture.

McBride's expression shifted and he stepped back from her, looking away. "Where's the bread?"

She waved her hand toward the bread box and retreated to the kitchen table. "Has Mr. Walters had a chance to hear the tape?" she asked.

"He didn't recognize the voice."

"Why'd the kidnapper call me? I just met Andrew Walters a couple of days ago. Abby isn't even in my class at school." She allowed herself a quick peek at McBride.

He put bread out on the counter and quickly started making a sandwich. "Good question. Any ideas?"

The hard tone of his voice made her wince inwardly. "No."

He set the sandwich on a napkin in front of her and took the chair opposite.

"Not eating?" she asked.

"Not hungry." He cocked his head, pinning her to her chair with the force of his gaze. She stared back at him, her breath trapped in her chest.

His features were too rough-hewn to be considered handsome. But he had amazing eyes, intense, clear and commanding. Their color shifted with his moods, almost brown when he was lost in thought, nearly green when he was working up a rage.

She wondered what color they turned in the heat of passion.

Trying to shake off the effect he'd begun to have on her, Lily leaned toward him across the table. "You obviously have questions for me. Let's have 'em."

"You had another vision?" His voice had a rumbling quality that made the skin on the back of her neck quiver. "Of Abby?"

She struggled to concentrate. "Yes. I think she was in a mobile home. The windows had metal frames and sills. And the room was tiny, with that boxy, prefab look some trailers have."

His gaze was dark and intense, impossible to read. "Anything that would help us identify it?"

"No. I only saw one room, and it was…ordinary." Though she tried to drop her gaze, she found herself unable to look away from him. He had a commanding quality about him, an air of strength and capability that elicited a primal response deep inside her.

It had been a long time since a man had made her feel this much like a woman. Why did it have to be McBride?

When he didn't respond right away, she felt herself begin to squirm, like a suspect under interrogation. She was pretty sure that was the point of his continuing silence.

"There was one thing—" She clamped her mouth shut before she revealed the odd appearance of the second girl. McBride obviously didn't believe she was having visions of Abby. Lily wasn't going to make things worse by mentioning a second child.

"One thing?" he prodded when she didn't continue.

"She talked to me this time."

He pulled back, his eyebrows twitching upward.

"I know it sounds crazy, but she heard me. She talked back. That's never happened before." Maybe because Lily had spent most of her life running from the visions, she'd never really explored the limits of her ability. She still couldn't think of it as a gift, not like her sisters'.

"You get migraines when you have visions?"

"Except when I don't fight them."

He picked up a pencil and grabbed a fresh sheet of paper. He jotted something on the page in his tight, illegible scrawl. "That's right. You mentioned something like that before you zoned out."

"Before I had a vision."

"Uh, yeah." He twirled the pencil between his fingers. "You said you fight them because they scare you."

She swallowed hard. "Yes."

"How long have you been having visions?"

"Of Abby?"

He shook his head. "In general."

"Since I was little." The visions had been part of her life for as long as she could remember.

"And you've always had headaches?"

"Not always." Before her father died, she'd never had

the headaches. But before then, she'd never had to fear her visions, either. "When I was younger, I didn't have headaches. But I didn't know to fight the visions."

For the first time he looked genuinely surprised. "They didn't scare you then? Why not?"

A flash of blood on jagged steel flashed through her mind. She closed her eyes, pushing it down into the dark place inside her. "I hadn't seen the bad things yet."

"Like what?" His voice lowered to a murmur. "Monsters?"

Was he making fun of her? He looked serious, so she answered. "I see people hurt. Killed. People in pain."

People like her father, bleeding to death on a bed of bloodstained sawdust…

"How do you know you don't have headaches when you don't fight the visions?"

"I had one the other day and didn't fight it. I didn't have any pain at all."

He cocked his head. "How can you know that's why?"

She sighed. "I suppose I can't. Does it matter? I'm going to keep trying to have them even if they hurt."

"Why would you put yourself through that?"

"Because Abby's still alive. I can still help her."

McBride looked at Lily for a tense moment. "Why are you having visions of Abby Walters? Why you in particular?"

"I don't know." The suspicion in his voice made her stomach cramp.

"When did they start?"

"Friday, at the school." The memory of those first brief glimpses of Abby remained vivid. Frightened blue eyes. Tearstained cheeks. Tangled red hair. A terrified cry.

"Did you have the vision before or after you talked to me?" McBride touched the back of her hand, trailing his fingers over her skin, painting her with fire.

She swallowed with difficulty, resisting the urge to beg him to touch her again. "Before."

A muscle in his jaw twitched. "How soon before?"

"Just before, I guess."

He met her gaze for a long, electric moment, his eyes now a deep forest-green. "What did you see that first time?"

She related the brief snatches of that vision, then told him about later seeing Abby in the car. "I think they were moving her to wherever they are now."

He tapped his fingers on the table mere inches from her hand. She watched them move, wishing they would touch her again. Her fingers itched to close the distance between them, but she resisted, forcing herself to look up at him, away from that tempting hand. But the smoldering emerald of his eyes did little to cool the heat starting to build inside her.

She licked her lips and tried to focus. "Is it against the rules for you to tell me how Abby's mother died?"

He didn't answer.

"I don't need details, I just..." She sighed, trying to explain the sensations she'd felt when talking to the kidnapper. "The man who called was desperate. I know he made a ransom demand, and maybe that's what they wanted all along. But I don't think they originally planned on a ransom call."

McBride cut his eyes toward her.

"He sounded scared. This wasn't how it was supposed to happen. Mrs. Walters wasn't supposed to die."

He caught her wrist. "Why do you say that?" His voice was tinged with suspicion, his eyes turning mossy brown.

"She fought, right?" Lily couldn't say how she knew that, but she did. "They didn't think she'd fight them. Maybe they don't have children of their own and don't know what a mother will do when her child's in danger."

He let go of her, but the heat of his touch lingered. She rubbed her wrist, trying to wipe away the tingling sensation his grip had imprinted in the tender flesh, as if every nerve ending had suddenly come alive. "That's how it happened, isn't it?" she asked.

He leaned toward her across the small table, close enough for her to breathe in his warm, spicy scent. "Why are you really interested in this case?"

She lifted her chin. "I keep seeing that scared little girl in my mind. I have to try to help her."

"You can't," he said bluntly.

"Why not?" she asked.

"Because she's already dead."

Sharp-edged and stone-cold, his words slammed into Lily like a physical blow. She shook her head. "That's not true. The kidnappers just called—"

"What makes you think it wasn't a crank call?"

"I recognized the voice."

"So you say."

Lily shut her eyes, wishing she could shut out his words as easily. "I know it was him."

"I've been a cop for sixteen years. I've investigated five nonparental child abductions over that time." Weariness crept into his matter-of-fact tone. "Kidnappers don't take five days to make a ransom call. They know it gives the cops too much time to get involved."

Lily opened her eyes but saw nothing but blackness. A soft, pain-wracked voice filled the darkness.

She's gone!

The darkness dissipated, the familiar decor of her kitchen coming back into focus, the echo of those two heartbroken words fading into the hum of the refrigerator behind her. Lily found McBride staring at her, his forehead creased with a frown.

He rose, his chair scraping against the tile floor. "I've put a patrol car outside to keep an eye on this place tonight. Tomorrow, with your permission, we'll tap your phone in case the man calls again." He didn't wait for her answer, making it halfway to the living room by the time Lily got her legs to work.

She followed him to the door, still shaking from the brief vision. Where had that woman's voice come from, pitched low with misery? Coming as it had in the wake of McBride's bitter words, was it connected to his own demons?

He had demons, without a doubt. Beneath his stony calm, Lily had sensed a misery so deep, so dark she could hardly bear to look at it.

She grabbed his arm as he opened the front door. "What if I don't want a tap on my phone?"

"Don't you want us to find out who's calling?" He stood close enough for her to see beard stubble shadowing his jaw. She could almost feel it, prickly against her skin, as if he'd rubbed his face against hers. His pupils were black pools rimmed by moss. Pure female response snaked through her belly, settling low and hot at her center.

"I'd also like to tap your cell phone," he added softly.

Right. Tapping the phone. "It's not listed anywhere by my cellular company. But you can tap my home phone."

He didn't look happy, but he didn't press the issue. He stepped away from her and onto her front stoop, robbing her of his warmth. Her strength seeped away, leaving her enervated and bone-weary.

He turned back to her, danger glittering in his murky eyes. "You're playing a reckless game, Ms. Browning. Take care."

She watched him stride down the walk, his jacket flapping in the cool night breeze, every heavy thud of her heart echoing his solemn warning. The intent of his words may have been different than her own interpretation, but the truth remained: the people who had Abby knew who Lily was and where she lived.

She wasn't safe in her own home.

Chapter Six

Andrew Walters was on his cell phone when Lily arrived at his hotel suite Thursday afternoon for their rescheduled meeting. He took her raincoat and waved her in, slanting her a rueful look as he spoke into the receiver. "We'll have to blow that one off. The county party chairman will understand." He gestured at the sofa, moving into one of the rooms off the main living area to complete his call.

Lily bypassed the sofa and walked to the picture window spanning one wall of the living area. During the day, the McMillan Place penthouse suite would boast a panoramic view of the lush woodlands west of town, but rain and falling darkness turned the window into a mirror reflecting Lily's own bedraggled image back at her. She patted her rain-curled hair and straightened her skirt, wishing she looked more presentable.

It was important that Andrew Walters believe what she had to tell him.

He returned to the room, flashing an apologetic smile. "That was my campaign manager, Joe. We have to figure out how to manage the campaign while all of this is going on."

Lily tried to hide her surprise. She'd have thought the election would be the last thing on Andrew's mind.

"You think that's cold of me." He sounded resigned.

"No," she replied.

"People have invested a lot of time and money in my campaign. For their sakes, I have to go through the motions." He beckoned for her to join him in the sitting area. "It's good to have something constructive to focus on, to keep my mind away from the worst possibilities."

She sat where he indicated. "Understandable."

He sank into an armchair and slanted a considering look at her. "The FBI told me about the call from the kidnapper. Why do you think he called you?"

If Andrew Walters harbored the same suspicions as Lieutenant McBride, he hid it well. He looked desperate and anxious, but he didn't seem distrustful.

Lily wished she had a better answer for both of them. "I guess they saw my picture in the paper. From the funeral. My name was in the caption, and I don't imagine there are that many Lily Brownings listed in the Borland phone book." It was the only explanation that made sense.

"I wonder how the press got your name in the first place."

She cocked her head. "I assumed you gave it to them."

"No." His eyes narrowed. "Probably Blackledge. He knew people would see us together and make assumptions. 'Andrew Walters didn't even let his first wife's body get cold before he found someone else.'"

She grimaced. "People won't think that."

He gave her a look that made her feel very naive.

She shook her head, appalled. "If my being there—"

"This is politics. Dirt gets flung. I'm becoming a little

better at ducking these days." His face tightened with anxiety. "McBride says you've had visions of my daughter. What did you see?"

She told him what she'd seen in her visions, holding back only the appearance of the second little girl. Andrew Walters listened, his hands clenched in his lap, his sharp-eyed gaze moving over her face as if gauging her veracity. "What was she wearing?" he asked when she finished.

For a second, Lily's mind went blank. She remembered so much about Abby—the way she smelled, the tear tracks down her dirty, freckled face, the way one red curl hung just off center over her forehead. But what she was wearing?

Lily closed her eyes, recreating the most vivid scene, the one where Abby had been huddled in the back of the moving car. She heard the hum of the motor, smelled the musty odor of the blanket under which the child had crouched, cold and afraid. She saw the messy red curls, the chattering teeth.

The light blue overalls with a yellow rabbit on the front.

"Overalls." Her voice shook. "Pale blue with a yellow bunny on the bib. And she had a long-sleeved white turtleneck underneath."

When Lily looked up, Andrew's face had gone pale. His voice shook when he spoke. "My God, you *did* see her."

She released a shaky breath. She'd been afraid she was wrong, that her visions really were delusions, as McBride apparently thought. "That's what she was wearing?"

The man nodded, color slowly seeping back into his face. "A neighbor who saw her Friday morning remembered the outfit. She'd bought it for Abby on her last birthday."

"So you believe me?"

Andrew reached across the space between them and took her hand. His expression solemn, he nodded. "I believe you."

Relief swamped her. "Mr. Walters, I'll do whatever I can to help you."

He managed a smile. "Thank you. And please, call me Andrew."

She nodded. "Andrew—"

The shrill ring of the telephone interrupted her, the sound jarring her spine.

"The dedicated line." Andrew's voice sounded strangled.

"Answer it," she urged, breathless. Her nerves were so taut that she didn't recognize the signs until gray mist invaded the edge of her vision.

As the fog thickened, she glimpsed a man hunched over a phone in a dim room. She barely made out dark green walls and a computer nearby. The man's blond hair was thin and patchy, and his skin was milky pale. The glow of the computer screen made twin blue squares on the lenses of his wire-rimmed glasses.

It was the caller, she realized when he spoke.

"Mr. Walters, listen quick." Lily was certain she'd never heard the voice before. It definitely wasn't the harsh-voiced man who'd hit Abby, the one who'd called her home on Wednesday.

"Who is this?" Andrew demanded.

"We have your daughter."

"Is Abby there?" Andrew's voice was like a fly buzzing in her ear, oddly unreal, even though he was in the same room with her. "Let me speak to her!"

"You have until tomorrow afternoon to get five hundred grand together. When you do that, you'll talk to your kid. Got it? And if you call the cops, you'll never see your kid again." The caller shifted, his desk chair creaking.

Beyond him, Lily saw a bed with rumpled green sheets. A newspaper lay near the pillows. Abby Walters's freckled face stared up from its front page. But there was no sign of Abby. And the room didn't remotely resemble the one where she'd seen the little girl in her visions.

"I'll call back tomorrow to tell you where to drop the money." The caller's hand shook as he clutched the phone.

He's not one of the kidnappers, Lily thought. *They know not to call Andrew Walters directly.*

She struggled against the swallowing mists, trying to slam shut the door of her mind. She'd seen all she needed to see. She had to tell Mr. Walters what she knew.

She emerged with a jolt when he banged the telephone receiver into its cradle and bent over the table, sucking in several deep, steadying breaths.

Lily stumbled to the couch and sat, pressing her hand to her head. Fighting to end the vision before it was finished had a price; colorful lights crowded her vision, and the first twinge of pain shot up from the base of her skull. She fumbled in her purse for her pills and swallowed one dry, laying her head back against the sofa cushions.

Andrew turned to face her. "He wouldn't let me talk to her." Anxiety creased his handsome face.

"He doesn't have her." Lily lifted her eyes to meet his, hating to burst his tiny bubble of hope. She told him what she could remember about the vision. "It was a hoax. I'm sorry."

Andrew sank to the sofa next to her and buried his face

in his hands. She touched his shoulder, unsure how to comfort him.

Someone rapped on the door. Andrew went to let two detectives into the room. "He wasn't on long enough for a trace, and his caller ID's blocked," one of them said.

Lily was no longer listening. She drifted on a river of pain, barely aware of the voices of the detectives talking or the trill of Andrew's cell phone when his campaign manager called back. Andrew's voice faded as he took the call in another room.

She wasn't sure how much time passed before a new voice roused her from her pain-washed daze. She struggled up from the depths of the soft couch and opened her eyes.

Detective McBride's stormy eyes stared back.

McBride crouched in front of Lily, trying to be angry. But she looked ready to collapse. Purple smudges bruised her eyes—headache, he guessed. "Walters says you think it's a hoax."

She hugged herself. The room was warm, but chill bumps dotted her bare arms. "I wish he'd kept that to himself."

"Why?" McBride lowered his voice to a gentle murmur.

Her eyes narrowed. "Aren't you angry I'm here?"

Tiny lines etched the skin around her eyes and mouth. Pain lines. He couldn't stop himself from touching a tiny crease in her forehead, gently smoothing it. "You have a headache?"

Her eyes drifted closed and she nodded, turning her head to give his fingers better access. Her body arched toward him, like a kitten responding to a gentle caress.

He dropped his hand with difficulty. "What did you do, fight your vision?"

Her eyes fluttered open. "I wanted to tell Andrew Walters about the hoax as quickly as possible." She stumbled over some of the words, as if she couldn't quite make them all fit together. "I fought to leave the vision before it was through."

And paid the price, he thought, then chided himself for letting himself get sucked into her delusion. Whatever had caused her headache, it damn well wasn't a psychic vision.

But she was right about the call being a hoax. Though smart enough to block his caller ID and keep his call too short for a trace, the man had blown it by not getting his business done in one shot.

Tomorrow he'd phone back and they'd get him.

"Can I go home now?" Lily leaned forward, bracing her hands on the sofa cushion. McBride stood to give her room to rise, but she moved faster than he did. Their bodies touched for a long, electric moment before he backed out of her way.

Maybe she *was* a witch, he thought, his body responding to her presence like fire to oxygen. He seemed entirely at her mercy, no matter how he tried to fight it. "Are you okay to drive?"

"I'm fine. The medicine's already working. And don't worry, officer. It's the non-drowsy formula." She gazed up at him, her eyes wide and glowing in the lamplight. Her body swayed toward him before she pulled herself up and slid past him, moving toward the door. McBride remained where he was, watching with clenched jaw as Andrew Walters closed his hand around Lily's arm and bent toward her, their faces intimately close as they spoke. Walters's grasp on Lily's arm became a gentle stroking, almost like a lover's caress.

McBride's chest tightened with anger.

"Lieutenant?"

McBride tore his attention away from Lily and Walters to look at the detective who'd contacted him after the call.

"Do you want to take the tape with you or do you want me to bag it and send it by courier?" the detective repeated.

"Courier," McBride answered.

As the two technicians headed out, McBride's eyes swung back to the door.

But Lily was gone.

He crossed to Walters. "You okay?"

Walters blinked as if startled. "Yeah. It's all just so crazy. Some creep playing with our minds." He shook his head. "How could someone do that?"

It's a big, bad world out there, McBride thought. Bigger and badder all the time. "We can't be sure it's a hoax."

"Lily's sure of it. That's good enough for me."

McBride's stomach sank as he dropped his hand from the other man's shoulder. "You know, Mr. Walters, we can't know for certain without a thorough investigation. I know Ms. Browning seems confident of everything she says, but—"

"She doesn't seem confident. I'd worry more if she did. But she's been right about everything so far."

"Like what?"

"She knew what Abby was wearing the day she disappeared."

McBride shook his head. "That was reported in the paper."

"Not the yellow rabbit."

"She knew about the rabbit?" Acid gushed into McBride's gut. The police had released a description of Abby's clothing—the blue overalls and white shirt—but held back the yellow rabbit decal to divide the crank calls from the genuine tips.

If Lily Browning had really described what Abby had been wearing, there was only one way she could have known.

She'd seen Abby Walters the morning she disappeared.

And he'd just let a person of interest walk out the door.

Chest tight with growing anger, McBride moved toward the exit. "I'm going to head out now and let our technicians handle things. Are you going to be okay?"

Walters looked exhausted. "I just want my daughter back."

"We'll find her." McBride heard the words, recognized his own voice, but couldn't believe what he'd said. He'd been raging at Lily Browning for giving Walters false hope, and here he was, adding his own lies to the mix.

He didn't believe the real kidnappers would call again, because Abby Walters was dead. Too much time had passed, with no sightings, and no clues but a harsh voice on Lily Browning's answering machine. Who knew whether that phone call was the real thing or just another of Lily's lies?

But he couldn't say that to Walters. Not yet. The man had to go through this part of the journey, the hopeful part. Next would come uncertainty, then despair, then the black anger that churned in the gut like a feeding frenzy of piranhas.

McBride didn't know what came after that.

AVOIDING THE CONGESTED perimeter highway, Lily took Black Creek Road home. It was a longer drive, but the winding road was lightly traveled, especially on a rainy night, and Lily was in no state of mind to deal with heavy traffic.

At least the migraine was almost gone.

But McBride's touch lingered like a fiery brand on her skin. She could still conjure up the tang of his aftershave, the intensity of his gaze sweeping over her as if he wanted to strip her bare of her defenses and find out what lay underneath.

Idiot. Trying to guess McBride's thoughts was a fool's game. If he thought of her at all, it was as a calculating con artist taking advantage of a wealthy but vulnerable man.

Whimsy wasn't Lily's style. She wasn't the fanciful sister; that was Rose, the hopeless romantic. She wasn't impulsive and daring like Iris, either. Lily was the eldest, the one with her head screwed on firmly. The one who'd taken care of her younger sisters when their mother died six years ago.

Lily didn't form ridiculous crushes on men who'd never return her feelings.

Mentally she dusted her hands of him. Done.

Her cell phone trilled, making her jump. She dug in her purse with her right hand and pulled out the phone. "Hello?"

"You never call, you never write." Her sister Rose's husky voice always reminded Lily of their mother. Iris, with her ebony hair and black-coffee eyes, looked the most like their mother, but Rose had her voice, low and just a little raspy, with a slow, sweet drawl that stretched her words like taffy.

"I talked to Iris just the other day."

"I always knew you liked her better," Rose said lightly. "I had a dream about you last night, Lil."

"Yeah?" Lily slowed her car as she approached Dead Man's Curve, where Black Creek Road formed a deep *S* as it followed the winding creek for a couple of miles.

"Yeah. Have you met a new man recently?"

McBride's rugged face flashed through mind. "Why?"

"Because you're going to fall in love with him."

A shiver ran down Lily's back. She ignored it, pressing her lips into a tight line. "Am not."

"Well, you also help him find his daughter. I'm not clear on whether you do that before you fall in love or after."

"Now I know you didn't dream that. Iris told you about my visions." Tucking her phone between chin and shoulder, Lily put both hands on the steering wheel as she navigated a sharp curve.

"Yes, she did, but I really did have the dream."

"Well, you're wrong on this occasion," Lily said firmly. "I've spent time with the little girl's father, and I assure you the last thing he's thinking about is falling in love."

Rose sighed. "It was a great dream. You were in the woods. There was a building with rickety wood steps. There he was—this incredible man, his arm around a little girl. He turned to look at you, and wow." Rose's voice dwindled to a contented sigh. "You were so in love with each other. It gave me chills."

Hair rose on the back of Lily's neck. If anybody but Rose were telling her these things, she'd laugh it off. But Rose's gift, predicting a successful love match, was as strong as Lily's, and much better developed. Still, Lily couldn't see herself with Andrew Walters. "What did this guy look like?"

"All I remember is dark hair."

"What about the girl?" Lily asked, thinking about Abby.

"I don't remember anything except she had big dark eyes that lit up when she saw you."

An image popped into Lily's head—of the dark-haired child at the edge of her vision of Abby. Lily shivered. Too creepy.

"So tell me about these visions you've been having."

Lily told her everything, including her newfound ability to make contact with Abby.

"She heard you? Cool! Any closer to finding her?"

Lily sighed. "I hope so. I'm worried, Rose. She's so scared. I feel helpless." She took a deep breath. "And during my last vision of Abby, I saw another little girl."

"The kidnappers have another little girl?" Rose asked.

"I don't think so. I think the little girl is somewhere else. Maybe nearby, though." Having spent so much of her life running from her visions, Lily had never figured out how they worked. Did the appearance of the new little girl have anything to do with Abby's kidnapping? Did the other child even exist, or was she a figment of Lily's imagination?

Maybe it was just a one-time thing. A fluke. Crossed wires or whatever you called mixed-up psychic signals.

"I've gotta run, Lil—Iris is in the cellar boiling her eye of newt and I think I just heard something explode." The humor in Rose's voice assured Lily that her baby sister was exaggerating. "Don't be a stranger, okay?"

Lily laughed. The sound startled her. How long had it been since she'd heard herself laugh? "If there's still a house left by the time you and Iris get through with it, I'll definitely be home for Thanksgiving."

As she ended the call with her sister, she noticed headlights flickering in her rearview mirror.

HE GRIPPED THE STEERING wheel, his palms sweating inside his leather driving gloves. In the darkness ahead, all he could see of Lily Browning's car was a pair of taillights glowing like red eyes. He pressed the accelerator to the floor, eating up the road between them.

She knew too much. Saw too much.

She would ruin everything.

He was close enough to make out the shiny chrome bumper of her Buick and the rectangular sticker with Westview Elementary School printed in white block letters on a field of red.

A schoolteacher, he thought. Panicked laughter rose in his throat. The most dangerous woman in his world was a bloody schoolteacher. How had this happened? How had everything gone so wrong so quickly?

No matter. It was going to end here.

Now.

WITH THE ON-RAMP to the perimeter highway backed up for more than a block, McBride went with a hunch and took Black Creek Road to avoid the snarl of traffic. If he was lucky, Lily Browning had taken the highway and he'd be sitting at her house waiting for her when she arrived. If not, he had a good chance of catching up with her on the winding back road.

Grabbing his cell phone, he called Theo Baker's direct line. "Call a meeting of the task force for first thing in the morning. I've had a copy of the phone call couriered over—"

"Right here in my hot little hands."

"Great. Get tech services to make a copy for everyone on the task force. Let's see if anybody recognizes the voice."

"Still think it's a hoaxer?"

"Ninety-nine percent sure." *But it's that one percent that could bite you in the ass,* McBride thought as he ended the call.

The weather was worsening; fog rising to meet the pouring rain that was already cutting visibility to a few yards. McBride peered into the darkness, easing off the accelerator as he approached Dead Man's Curve. Rain sheeted across the blacktop and pounded his windshield, keeping pace with the wipers.

Ahead, two glowing red dots pierced the gloom. Taillights, he realized. Lily's car? Accelerating, he kept his eyes on the lights. As the road straightened for a long stretch, the taillights doubled. He squinted, trying to make sense of what he was seeing. Now two sets of lights traveled side by side on the two-lane road. One car passing a slower one?

Suddenly, both cars jerked violently to the right. His heart sped up. Was that a collision?

His cell phone trilled, sending his taut nerves jangling. He grabbed it and thumbed the talk button. "McBride."

"Lieutenant, this is Alli with Dispatch. You asked us to flag any call that came in from cell phone number 555-3252."

Lily's number.

"We've got a Lily Browning on with a 911 operator. She says another car is trying to run her off the road."

"What's her twenty?" On the road ahead, the pairs of taillights took another jarring lurch to the right.

"Black Creek Road, a mile before Five Mile Crossing."

McBride's heart jolted into high gear. He jammed his foot on the accelerator, ignoring the shimmy of the Chevy's tires on the slick blacktop.

Suddenly, the taillights ahead disappeared from view. McBride's breath caught. It took a second to realize the dispatcher was calling his name. "Yeah?"

"Sir, we just lost contact."

Chapter Seven

Lily threw her dead cell phone into the passenger seat, wishing she'd plugged the adapter into the cigarette lighter before she'd left McMillan Place. At least she'd managed to give her location to the operator before her phone went dead.

Gripping the steering wheel, she braced as the car beside her slammed into her again, sending her sliding toward the shoulder. She steered with the skid, managing to right the car before it went over the drop off into the thick woods.

With no streetlamps on the lonely stretch of road, she could make out little about the other car or its driver. It was a dark sedan, an older model judging by its shape, with tinted windows that hid the occupant from view. Not being able to see who was driving her off the road only amplified her terror.

What if her assailant rammed her down the steep embankment into the trees? Would another passing driver be able to see her vehicle from the road? And what would her attacker do if she was trapped and vulnerable at the bottom of the embankment?

She couldn't help but think of Debra Walters and Abby, alone on a stretch of desolate road, with nothing to protect them from the carjackers but Debra's willingness to defend her daughter to the death.

Was the person behind those tinted windows the harsh-voiced man from her vision? He knew where she lived; could he have followed her to McMillan Place, waiting to make his move?

Around another curve, her headlights outlined the concrete rails of a bridge spanning a narrow gorge. Lily didn't have to be psychic to know the other driver would double his efforts to send her off the road once they reached the bridge. And if she went over the side into the creek, she'd never survive the fall.

She sped up as she hit the bridge, praying her tires would grip the slick pavement long enough to get her safely to the other side. Her acceleration caught her tormenter by surprise, forcing him to gun his engine to keep from falling behind.

Lily's tactic gave her enough of an edge to cross the bridge unmolested, but as she reached solid ground again, the dark sedan bumped against the back panel of her Buick and veered hard to the right. She had no chance to recover as her assailant's maneuver sent her car spinning across the slippery road.

She held on, trying to keep from sliding over the opposite shoulder, but the momentum was uncontrollable. The world became a blur of dark and light as the Buick hit the shoulder and lurched backward down the fifteen-foot embankment, crashing into a tree with a bone-jarring crunch.

Lily's head whipped forward and slammed back into

the headrest, setting off a brief fireworks display behind her eyes. When the lights and colors faded, she forced herself to shake off the shock and take stock of her condition.

The trunk of the Buick had taken most of the impact of the collision with the tree, leaving the front part of her car in pretty good shape. Her airbag hadn't deployed, though her seat belt had done its job, holding her in place while her car plunged off the road. She'd be feeling the bruises from the shoulder strap for days, and her headache was back with a vengeance. Beyond that, all her moving parts worked and she hadn't really lost consciousness.

Shaking wildly, she cut the engine. Her windshield wipers stopped at half-mast, their rhythmic swish-swish abruptly silenced. The void was filled by the heavy drumbeat of rain on the roof and the low moan of wind in the trees behind her, a lonesome sound that amplified her sense of vulnerability tenfold.

She peered through the water sheeting on her windshield, trying to see the road. The maneuver that sent her spinning had been a risky move for the other car. Had it met its own fate on the opposite side of the road?

She leaned over and opened the glove compartment, scrabbling through the contents until she found the cell phone adapter. She'd feel safer once she got the 911 operator back on the phone.

But when she finally located her cell phone on the floorboard on the passenger side, its plastic skin lay cracked and askew, wires spilling out through the opening.

Thank God she'd already called for help before the phone went dead. But it would take time for anyone to find her on the long stretch of winding road. And if her attacker hadn't spun out the way she had—

Light suddenly slanted across her windshield, splintered into glittering facets by the driving rain. She peered through the downpour, her heart in her throat.

Two powerful beams sliced through the gloom at the top of the embankment. They were steady and stationary.

Whoever it was had parked on the shoulder.

Panic zigzagged through her belly. What should she do? Stay put? Try to get out and hide in the woods?

She couldn't risk the former; she might as well be a rat in a cage, waiting to be fed to a snake. Her shoes weren't made for trekking through the forest, but she didn't have to survive out there for long. She just had to hope help arrived before her assailant found her.

Opening her door was harder than she'd expected; the car had sunk into the mud, leaving precious little room to maneuver.

She squeezed through the opening, grabbing her raincoat as she stumbled through the sucking mud. She lost a shoe right off and had to waste time retrieving it, crouching low in hopes that the occupant of the car above hadn't spotted her yet in the foggy darkness.

She took off the other shoe and squished across the soggy ground until she was well hidden in the trees. Flattening herself against the rough bark of a towering pine, she peeked back up at the roadway.

A dark figure stood at the edge, his large body backlit by the high beams. He seemed to be gazing down toward her car, his hands curled into fists. Then he began loping down the embankment, taking little care as he slipped and slid on the slick grass.

She could make out only his shadow now, large and looming, so close that she could hear the ragged hiss of his breathing. Terror coiled like a viper in the pit of her belly, spreading poison until her body froze with fear.

When he jerked the driver's door open, the glow of her dome light rimmed his profile, revealing the familiar set of a square jaw and tension lines carved on either side of his mouth.

Her knees buckling with relief, Lily dug her fingers into the pine bark to keep from sliding to the ground. A soft whimper escaped her throat as a splinter dug into her palm. "McBride."

He whirled around, peering into the woods. "Lily?"

She willed her legs to hold her upright for the few uneven steps it took to reach the clearing where McBride stood. She couldn't see his expression, now that the light was at his back again, but she heard his soft exhalation, saw his shoulders sag for a second before he closed the distance between them in two long strides and gathered her into his arms.

She wrapped hers around his neck as he lifted her out of the wet grass and into his tight embrace. His pulse hammered against her breast, keeping pace with her own racing heart.

"Are you hurt?" He started to release her, but she tightened her grip around his neck, shaking her head. He lifted one hand to tangle in her hair, brushing the rain-drenched mass away from her face.

"Are you sure?"

She nodded. "I'm going to be a little sore, I think. But nothing permanent."

He glanced over his shoulder at her battered car, then

back at her. Now that her eyes were adjusting to the darkness, she could see the angry set of his jaw and the glitter of leashed violence in his eyes. "Who did this? Did you get a look at him?"

She tried to gather her wits, though the combination of delayed reaction and McBride's hard body pressed against hers made coherent thought difficult. "It was a dark four-door sedan with tinted windows. I couldn't see the driver at all."

He uttered a terse profanity. "I saw it happening—I was about a quarter mile back when he started ramming you. But I couldn't catch up in time."

"That was you?" The lights in her rearview mirror. The ones that had given her hope for a brief moment. She pressed her forehead against his throat, her fingers digging into the muscles of his shoulders as she realized just how easily her fate could have gone the other way.

"Did you see what happened to the other car?"

"All I saw was his taillights ahead. He must have spotted me coming, and gunned it. When I saw the skid marks on the grassy shoulder here, I stopped to see if you were hurt." He ran his thumb down her cheek, letting it settle at the edge of her lower lip. His voice softened. "You're trembling."

She was. And as much as she'd like to attribute it to shock, the main thing sending shivers down her spine was McBride's body pressed hard and hot against hers.

His gaze dipped to her parted lips, his breath quickening. She could see the struggle on his face, the need to resist. The sharp edges of her own doubts nicked her conscience even as she lifted her chin and met his mouth halfway.

Fire raced through her veins, surprising her with its wild intensity. McBride's arm tightened around her back, pulling her closer. His other hand tangled in her wet hair, curling into a fist until she was ensnared in his grasp.

He took his time with the kiss, giving and demanding in equal parts, stoking the flames in her belly. His tongue brushed over her lower lip, tasting her. Teasing her.

A low moan of pleasure rumbled up her throat. He tightened his arms around her in response, lifting her off her feet. One hand slid down her back, settling low, pressing her hips firmly against the hard ridge of his erection. Heat flooded her, settling at her center, warming her from the inside out.

He lifted his mouth away only long enough to blaze a trail across her jawline and down the side of her throat, nipping and kissing a path across her collarbone. She melted against him, a shimmering onslaught of need flooding her veins.

At the first faint sound of sirens in the distance, she tightened her hold on his shoulders, not ready to let him go. But he broke the contact, gently setting her back on her feet and taking a step away, breathing hard and fast. His gaze locked with hers, wary and oddly vulnerable, as the sound of sirens grew, piercing the drumbeat of rain.

After an endless moment, he held out his hand. "Think you can make it back to the road if I help you?"

Nodding, she grasped it, wondering if he could feel the tremors still fluttering through her from the kiss.

His big palm enclosed hers. "Need anything from the car?"

"My purse."

He let go long enough to retrieve the bag, and handed it to her. Then he took her hand again and helped her up the steep incline.

As they reached the road, a police car and an EMT unit were pulling up behind McBride's idling car. The two medics immediately took charge, separating her from McBride and helping her onto a stretcher in the back of the truck while they looked her over for any possible injuries. She leaned forward to peer around them, not ready to let McBride out of her sight.

He stood a few feet away, bathed in a wide shaft of golden light pouring from the EMT vehicle. He met her gaze with a reassuring smile before moving away to talk to the uniformed officers waiting by his car.

She sank back on the stretcher and closed her eyes, her mouth still tingling from McBride's kiss.

MCBRIDE'S WATCH READ four-fifteen when he woke in the predawn gloom of Lily Browning's living room. Her sofa was built for a woman, sturdy enough but small. Cozy. Definitely not the ideal bed for a man of his size.

The EMTs had reassured him that the purple marks from the seat belt were superficial. Lily had been a little shocky, but a hot shower, dry clothes and extra blankets on her bed had fixed that.

She'd fallen asleep in his car on the way home and had roused only long enough to shower and crawl into bed. When he'd checked on her a little after nine, she'd been fast asleep.

Rubbing the ache in his neck, McBride let his eyes adjust to the pale glow of light from a streetlamp seeping through the thin curtains on Lily's front windows. He stretched his legs out in front of him, trying to find a more comfortable position.

He shouldn't have stayed. A police car was parked

outside, manned by two perfectly capable officers. Hanging around all night was overkill.

Not to mention dangerous.

He'd kissed her. Not a gentle, comforting peck on the cheek to reassure her that she was safe, either. No, he'd gone for long, wet and greedy.

Worse still, she'd tasted just as he'd expected—sweet with a tangy edge, like wild honey. The curves and planes of her body had fit perfectly against his, soft and hot despite the cold rain drenching them both.

How had he let this happen? Even now he felt the tug of her calling to him, just beyond the closed door at the end of the hall. If he went to her bed, would she turn him away?

He rubbed the heels of his palms against his bleary eyes. He was insane. She was a suspect, for God's sake! The attack on her tonight didn't change the fact that she had information only the kidnappers and cops should have. How did she know what Abby had been wearing the day she disappeared?

Maybe she really did see Abby in her mind, a treacherous voice inside him whispered.

No. He knew better than that. He'd learned that lesson the hard way. But could the trembling woman who'd returned his kiss with a sweet passion that made his head spin really be involved with murder and kidnapping?

He sat forward, burying his head in his hands. The idea seemed almost as insane as the alternative.

But those didn't have to be the only choices, did they?

Maybe the truth lay somewhere in between.

LILY CURLED UP IN BED with her cats, somewhere between sleep and wakefulness. Though sleep had done wonders for her, she felt sore all over from her nerve-wracking ordeal. And below the twinges and aches lay a relentless hum of awareness, a disturbing reminder of how her world had tilted upside down again with one shattering kiss.

Why in the world had she let herself lose control that way? She couldn't trust McBride; he still thought she was involved in Abby Walters's kidnapping. Lily had seen it in his eyes the day before in Andrew's hotel suite. And even if his doubts hadn't built an impenetrable wall between them, the man himself posed a grave danger to her heart.

The more she learned about the detective, the less she knew. He was a man steeped in secrets. Terrible ones, if the darkness she'd felt from him that night in her kitchen meant anything. What if being around him opened her mind to whatever horrors lurked within him? Could she bear it?

She shivered, cold despite the blankets piled atop her. Delilah nestled closer, a hot little knot against her side, but the shivers grew stronger. The darkness of the bedroom had already begun changing color and texture before Lily realized that she was having another vision.

She opened the door in her mind, both eager and afraid to see what lay beyond. As she pushed forward through the thick fog, she felt a warning pain behind her eyes and forced herself to let the vision flow around her, carrying her at its own pace.

Eventually the mists cleared to reveal Abby Walters lying on the lumpy bed where Lily had found her in her last vision. The child slept fitfully, her pale eyelids twitching with a dream. She looked cleaner than before. Lily took a deep breath through her nose and smelled soap.

Somebody had given Abby a bath, she thought with faint relief. Maybe that meant they were trying to take care of her.

Unless…

A darker thought forced her mind to a horrible place. Abby, naked and vulnerable in the hands of the man—men?—who had brutally killed her mother. Nausea rose in Lily's throat, making her eyes sting with acrid tears.

"What did they do to you, baby?" She stroked Abby's cheek, her fingers tracing damp tear tracks.

"It's okay," a child's voice whispered, very close.

Lily whirled around.

The dark-haired girl from her earlier vision stood behind her, clad in yellow-striped pajamas a size too small for her. She clutched a ragged stuffed toy against her chest, something round and tattered, its furry green body worn and thin.

She smiled tentatively at Lily. "I watched her for you."

Chapter Eight

Lily felt as if she'd gone mad. "You watched her?"

The little girl nodded. "I know you can't always be here, so I check on her sometimes to make sure she's okay."

Lily's mind reeled, threatening to suck her back to reality. She forced herself to stay calm, let the vision hold her in its gossamer web. "Who are you?"

"Mama calls me Gina, but I don't think that's my name. She's not really my mama, you know. My real mama's dead."

Lily noticed the little girl was almost transparent, unlike Abby. She wasn't actually in the same room, Lily realized. She was somewhere else.

But where?

"I can't stay much longer." The girl began to fade.

Lily reached out, wondering if she could touch her. "Wait, Gina! Are you sure Abby's okay?"

The girl's image rippled. "Yes."

Before Lily could move, the dark-haired girl was gone.

Lily slowly turned back to Abby. The child's eyelids had stopped fluttering and her soft, snuffling breath was even and deep. Relief trickled through Lily as she watched the child's peaceful slumber, until the fog began to swirl around her, drawing her back to the doorway.

She reached out to stroke Abby's cheek again before the door in her mind closed, hiding the child from her sight.

Emerging from the fog, Lily sat upright in the bed, hugging herself with trembling arms. The face of the dark-haired child remained etched in her mind, pale, heart-shaped, and so, so sad.

She shivered. Who was this solemn little girl?

BLUE MOONLIGHT BATHED the bedroom. The little girl blinked as she emerged from the haze to find herself huddled in bed.

She looked around quickly, just to reassure herself that she was back in her own room. She clutched Mr. Green more tightly to her, rubbing her cheek against his threadbare fur. Straining her ears, she listened for Mama. But the house was silent.

She pulled the covers more tightly around herself and stared at the cracked ceiling. She knew something was wrong with her mother. In her little-girl wisdom, she also knew Mama's trouble had something to do with her.

Mama called her Gina, but that wasn't her name. She was Casey. She had vague memories of someone calling her name. "Casey, baby, come here." The voice was deep. A man's voice. She liked the way it sounded, a little gruff but tender.

She knew the voice belonged to her daddy, but she barely remembered him. Only Mama, for just about as long as she recalled. The fuzzy memories that came at night, memories of being held in Daddy's strong arms, were little more than dreams.

Sweet dreams.

Nestled under the covers, Casey felt sleep creeping up on her. She closed her eyes, picturing Lily, the nice lady who was taking care of Abby. Casey smiled in the dark.

That smile carried her softly into sleep.

LILY OVERSLEPT, waking with bright morning sunlight slanting through her bedroom window. The digital alarm clock read seven twenty-five. She was going to be late for work.

She sat up quickly, gasping as pain rocketed through her entire body before settling in a hot ache in the back of her neck. Okay, work was out.

She reached for her phone and called Carmen Herrera's office number. "Carmen, it's Lily. I'm so sorry, I overslept and I haven't even had a chance—"

"Lily, thank God you're okay!" Carmen interrupted. "Lieutenant McBride called me this morning to let me know about the accident so I could arrange for a substitute for your classes. He said you were a little banged up."

Lily glanced at her reflection in the dresser mirror. Shadows circled her eyes, almost as dark as the vivid bruises slanting across her shoulder and chest where the shoulder belt had left its mark. "I'm a little bruised and sore, but I should be fine by Monday. Thanks for getting someone to fill in."

She hung up the phone and eased her sore legs over the edge of the bed. Jezebel glided in from the hall and wrapped herself around Lily's ankles, meowing.

"I bet you're hungry, aren't you, Jezzy?" She put on a

bathrobe and hobbled down the hall to the kitchen, wondering if McBride had already left for the office.

But he was waiting in her kitchen, the morning paper spread out in front of him, a mug of steaming coffee sitting to one side. He looked up when she entered. "The nice cat has been fed. The psycho one refused to eat anything I gave her."

Lily glanced at the four open cans of cat food on the counter, her lips curving with amusement.

She picked up the tuna, Jezebel's favorite, and emptied it in one of the cat bowls. Jezebel went straight to it and started eating.

"Spoiled brat," McBride murmured.

"Thank you for calling in for me." Lily poured herself a cup of coffee and joined McBride at the table before taking a sip. Strong and hot, the coffee burned going down, making her eyes water.

"I figured you'd be too sore from the accident to deal with a bunch of eight-year-olds." His gaze dropped to her throat. "Do those bruises hurt much?"

"Not too much." She lifted a hand to her neck. He was being too nice to her. It made her feel self-conscious.

"I hope you don't mind, but I found your sisters' phone number in your address book and called to let them know you'd been in an accident. I talked to the one named Rose."

Lily bit back a smile at the look on his face. Two minutes on the phone with Rose had probably confused the hell out of him. Her ebullient sister was Lily's polar opposite.

Her smile faded. It hadn't always been that way.

"She said she would be here before noon."

Lily frowned. "I don't need a babysitter."

His expression became shuttered. "She insisted. Besides, I've got to get out of here soon—I have a meeting at nine. I've called for a patrol to come by your house every thirty minutes, just in case there's any trouble."

She set her coffee cup down, her stomach clenching. "Are you expecting trouble?"

He gave her a considering look. "You tell me."

Ah, there was the McBride she knew. Suspicious by nature. "I didn't imagine the phone call from the kidnapper. You heard him. You also saw that car run me off the road. Unless you think I arranged that, too?"

His only answer was a slight narrowing of his eyes.

"Because it makes so much sense to risk life and limb on the off chance that you left Andrew Walters's hotel room right after I did, and took the same detour I took."

"Well, you do claim to be a psychic," he pointed out.

"I don't claim to *be* anything." She picked up her coffee cup and took it to the sink, emptying the dark liquid down the drain. She'd had about all she could take of McBride and his coffee for one day. "All I've ever said is that I see things other people don't."

"Potato, potah-to," he murmured in her ear.

She turned and found him inches away. "What do you want from me?" Her own voice came out soft as a whisper.

His half smile faded. "I want you to stay away from Andrew Walters. His life is turned upside down, and he's clinging to anything that'll make his world stop shaking. Including you."

"What are you suggesting?"

"Walters thinks you can find his daughter. That makes you the most important person in his life right now."

Lily frowned, not liking what he was implying. "Look, I know you didn't like finding me at Mr. Walters's hotel, but I assure you—"

"What do you think will happen to Walters if you don't deliver Abby in the end?" McBride asked.

A flicker of uncertainty ran through her. What if she couldn't? Was she giving the man false hope?

"You're telling Andrew Walters that his little girl is all right, that there's still a chance he'll find her again. Do you really know that?" McBride edged closer. "What happens if tomorrow we find Abby's body in a ditch somewhere? How much harder is that going to be for the man?"

Her throat tightened, his soft words painting vivid pictures in her mind. "Stop it."

McBride suddenly looked tired. "I don't mean to hurt you, Lily. But there are too damn many odds against her." His voice was so flat and faraway, she hardly recognized it. "So please, don't give Walters any false encouragement. Okay?"

"Am I supposed to pretend I never heard of Abby Walters?" Tears blurred Lily's vision. "She's a scared little girl who saw her mommy die, and now she's all alone with two very bad men. I won't abandon her in that dark place."

McBride took a deep breath. "Then come to me instead of Walters. Tell *me* about your visions."

Wariness flitted through her. "Tell you?"

"I promise I'll look into everything you tell me." He looked queasy, but his gaze remained steady.

"Mr. Walters expects me to stay in touch."

"I'll tell him you're part of my investigation and you'll be reporting to me now." McBride took a step back. "Deal?"

She licked her lips, realizing that he'd just played her—and that it had worked. She would do what he asked. "You won't ignore what I tell you?"

"I'll follow every lead you give me."

She put her hand over her mouth, wondering if she was making a mistake. But when she dropped her hand, it was to say, "Okay, it's a deal."

The look of satisfaction in his eyes made her immediately regret giving in so easily. But she quelled her doubts; she could always break her end of the deal if he broke his.

She released a pent-up breath. "So what do I do, call you if I have a vision? And I guess you'll want me to write down everything I see, right?"

He seemed flummoxed by the question, as if he hadn't quite thought past manipulating her into staying away from Andrew Walters. Beneath the confusion, a darker emotion burned in his narrowed eyes.

"Is something wrong?" she asked.

He shook his head. "Yes, write everything down."

Lily pushed her hair back from her face. "Is this going to be a problem for you?"

He lifted his gaze to meet hers, his expression shuttered. "No. No problem."

She studied his face, trying to figure out what he was thinking. He could hide his emotions as well as almost anyone Lily knew, although he couldn't quite cover up the dark place inside him. It roiled, black and deep, just under the surface.

He took a step toward the doorway. "I should go. I need to head home and change."

She walked him to the door, leaning against the jamb

as he took his jacket from the coat rack. He paused next to her, turning to meet her uplifted gaze.

"Call if you need me."

Heat bloomed deep in her belly. "I will."

He leaned in, and she rose on her toes to meet him halfway, as if drawn by a microscopic thread, the pull of his body intense and powerful. She curled her hand around his neck and brushed her lips against his. She'd expected combustion, but instead, the sweetness of the kiss washed over her in a river of warmth. She relaxed, giving in to the velvety caress of his mouth on hers.

When he gently broke away, coldness seeped into the marrow of her bones.

McBride stepped back onto the concrete stoop, gathering his coat around him to ward off the chill. Lily closed the door, needing the distance, the barrier between them.

But she remained there, her cheek against the door, long after she heard his car drive away.

ROSE ARRIVED AROUND TEN, laden with an overnight case, bran muffins and a thermos. "Iris sent buckbean tea." Rose hugged Lily. "You okay? McBride said you got a little banged up."

"I'm fine." Lily took the basket of muffins from her sister and led her inside. "My car's totaled, though."

Rose dropped her bag on the floor by the sofa and followed Lily to the kitchen. She glanced at the two coffee cups in the sink. "So, this McBride—is he cute?"

Lily put the muffins on the counter and gave her sister a warning look.

Rose bent and picked up Delilah, who had wound herself in a knot around her legs. "Hello, gorgeous." She rubbed the cat's ears until Delilah purred like a motorboat. "Iris would've come, but she's almost figured out some mix of bat's wings and eye of newt that'll relieve menstrual cramps in half the usual time, and far be it from me to stand in the way of such a miracle."

Lily pulled the plastic wrap off the basket and picked out a couple of muffins for herself and Rose. "Put my cat down and pour us some tea."

Rose poured two cups and joined Lily at the kitchen table, moving aside the newspaper McBride had left folded on the table. "So really—who is this McBride and why did he spend the night with you?"

Heat rushed up Lily's neck and spilled into her cheeks. She touched the edge of the newspaper at her elbow, trying to hide her reaction. But the paper only reminded her that McBride had sat here reading this paper only a few hours earlier, looking sleepy and disheveled and utterly irresistible.

"Ooh, Lil, you're blushing!" Rose leaned forward, her expression eager. "Spill it!"

Lily gave her sister a stern look. "McBride's the head of the task force investigating Abby Walters's abduction."

"Ooh, and you're working with him? Because of your visions?"

"Kind of." Lily caught her up with all that had happened since they'd spoken on the phone the night before.

Rose's eyes widened with horror. "Someone ran you off the road? McBride just said it was an accident."

"I don't know who it was or why he wanted to hurt me," Lily admitted. "It doesn't make any sense—the kidnapper who called me the other day seemed to want me to give Andrew a message. But maybe I spooked him when he realized I'd seen him hit Abby."

"Have you had more visions since then?"

"Yeah. A really strange one." Glad for a sympathetic ear, Lily told Rose about the second little girl who'd appeared in her visions of Abby. "It was so strange. It was like she'd been watching Abby and me."

Rose's eyes glittered. *"Creepy!"*

"It didn't feel creepy, though," Lily said. "At first, maybe, but after that it seemed sort of sweet. How she'd been watching over Abby."

"You think she knows Abby?"

"I think she's connected somehow. Maybe a cousin or something. Something about her looks familiar."

"Why would Abby's cousin come to you in a vision?"

Lily shrugged. "I'd love to ask Andrew Walters about the little girl, but I promised McBride I'd stay away from him."

Before Rose could respond, Jezebel jumped from the counter onto the kitchen table, knocking over Lily's tea.

"Jezzy!" Rose jumped up to avoid the liquid spreading toward her.

Lily shooed the cat away and crossed to the counter to retrieve a roll of paper towels to mop up the mess, while Rose grabbed the newspaper off the table to keep it from getting wet.

When Lily dumped the soaked towels and returned to the table, she found Rose gazing at the paper, a strange light in her eyes.

"What is it?" she asked.

Rose turned the paper around, showing Lily a front-page photo of McBride and a couple of detectives Lily didn't recognize, manning phones at police headquarters.

Rose pointed to McBride. "This is McBride, isn't it?"

Lily nodded, chill bumps rising on her arms. The picture caption didn't identify him by name. "How'd you know?"

Rose's grin split her face from ear to ear. "Sugar, he's the man you're going to marry."

Chapter Nine

McBride watched the cable news interview through narrowed eyes, a little unnerved by how well Andrew Walters was holding together under the camera lights. The man was smooth, well-spoken and engaging. The camera loved him.

No wonder he was in politics.

"I'm grateful for everyone's support. I can't tell you how much it means to me." Walters looked straight at the camera, his chin up, his eyes soft with emotion. "Please remember to keep your eyes open. Be aware of who's around you. That little redhead you see in the grocery store could be my daughter."

"He's good," FBI Special Agent Cal Brody murmured.

McBride glanced at the agent. Brody was a lean, rangy man with the sharp eyes of a hunter. He said little and missed nothing. And he looked just as bemused as McBride felt.

"He has an alibi," McBride responded, aware what the agent's dry words were implying. "And no discernible motive."

"What about his opponent?"

"If Blackledge was behind it, he screwed up. Walters's poll numbers are way up since his daughter disappeared." A niggle of unease crept under McBride's collar as he spoke.

"Motive." Brody echoed the path of McBride's thoughts.

McBride pressed his lips together, considering the idea of Walters as the mastermind behind his daughter's kidnapping. Was it possible? His alibi was airtight, so he'd have had to hire someone else to make the snatch…

No. Until this morning, when he'd arrived to find Walters up to his elbows in campaign discussions with his campaign manager, Joe Britt, McBride had never seen the man as anything other than a desperate, heartsick father.

But Walters had a job to do, just like McBride.

When Brody joined McBride and Walters that morning, he'd gone over the FBI's game plan. "We think we've figured out this guy's trace-blocking system, so we should be able to pinpoint him when he calls today. We get his location, we strike, we grab him." Brody had looked at Walters. "I understand you don't believe he's legitimate."

"Lily is sure he's a fraud," Walters had said.

"Lily?" Brody had asked.

"She's a psychic who's helping us find Abby," Walters had said before McBride could stop him. McBride had braced himself for the agent's reaction.

Brody's only response had been a quick glance at McBride.

Walters had managed to stay away from the topic of Lily for most of the day, distracted by a Birmingham television news crew who'd arrived to interview him about his missing daughter.

McBride wished he were as easily distracted. He couldn't seem to stop thinking about Lily Browning.

The crew wrapped up the interview, broke down their equipment and left. Walters went to change clothes, leaving McBride alone with Brody.

"How closely did you look at him?"

"Verified his alibi. Checked his bank account to see if there were any odd outputs of money, but he is in the middle of a senate run. There've been outlays. But they seem legit."

Brody shrugged. "From what I know about Blackledge, if Walters had any skeletons, they'd be out of the closet already."

Brody was right. Walters knew what it was like to live under scrutiny. It was only reasonable he'd hold up under pressure better than the average guy with a missing daughter.

Walters returned to the sitting room, minus his jacket and tie. "I hope that earns us a few more eyeballs."

Odd phrasing, McBride thought. But the trill of a phone diverted his attention.

It was the dedicated line.

McBride glanced at Brody. The fed nodded. Andrew Walters sank onto the sofa and took a deep breath.

As they'd agreed, McBride answered the phone. "Hello?"

"Hello, Mr. Walters. Remember me?"

McBride recognized the voice from the surveillance tape. He squeezed the receiver tightly. "I remember." He smoothed his gravelly voice to sound more like Walters.

"We want five hundred grand in tens and twenties, dropped in the waste bin at the corner of 10th and Maple.

Tomorrow night at eleven-thirty. We'll be watching, so don't be stupid."

"That's a lot of money to get together by then."

"Don't jerk me around, Walters. You're worth fifty times that. Eleven-thirty tomorrow night." The man's voice quavered despite his attempt to sound tough. "And no cops, got it? I smell so much as a whiff of bacon, the kid is dead."

McBride gritted his teeth. "You'll have Abby there?" He wondered if the FBI techs had been able to get a trace yet.

"Just be there." There was a click, then a dial tone.

A second later, an FBI surveillance tech burst through the door. "We've got him!"

LILY STARED AT HER SISTER. "I beg your pardon?"

"I said, you're going to marry McBride." Rose was matter-of-fact, as if she'd just said Lily was having waffles for breakfast. "I just now saw a true-love veil, your face over his. You know what that means."

Lily shook her head. No matter how attractive she found McBride, she couldn't believe he was her "one true love." They'd never find common ground enough to be together forever.

"He's the man in the dream I had, the man you're going to be madly in love with, remember? You find his daughter...." Rose stopped, frowning. "Does McBride have a daughter?"

"I don't think so." None she knew of, anyway. McBride wasn't the most forthcoming man she'd ever met. "I think you're off the mark this time." A queasy feeling settled in her stomach. "For all I know, he's happily married."

Which would shine a new, unwelcome light on their recent kisses, she realized with a sinking heart.

Rose frowned. "I'm never wrong about these things."

"Trust me, whoever the mystery man is, it's not McBride." She changed the subject. "How's business?"

"Pretty good. Right now I'm working on a wedding in Willow Grove and one over in Talladega. I think—"

The jangling phone interrupted her. Lily shrugged apologetically and answered on the second ring. "Hello?"

"Lily? It's Andrew Walters. They traced the call!"

Lily's stomach flipped. "Really?"

"I'm heading to the station to wait for them to arrive with the suspect." Andrew paused, tension buzzing over the phone line. "Are you sure he doesn't have Abby?"

About to reassure him, Lily remembered McBride's warning. What if she was wrong? What if she built up Andrew's hopes, only to have all her visions turn out to be nothing but delusions?

It didn't matter, she realized. "McBride won't let anything happen to Abby." He'd die before he'd let her get hurt. It was the one thing Lily was sure about.

"Will you come to the police station? I need you there."

Lily hesitated, remembering her promise to McBride. But she needed to be there. Already she was pumped with adrenaline; sitting here in ignorance for hours, waiting for news, would be too excruciating to contemplate. "On my way."

"Where're you going?" Rose asked when she hung up.

Lily explained briefly. "I have to go."

"We'll take my car," Rose said.

"We'll have to," Lily said, her hands trembling as she thought about what awaited her.

AS UNIFORMED OFFICERS pulled him from the back of the squad car, Ray Biddle squinted at McBride. "You got the wrong man."

McBride smiled grimly. "We always do." He followed the tight little procession into the booking area. As the clerks began to process Biddle, Theo Baker came around the corner. He crooked his palm at McBride, motioning him to follow.

"What's up?" McBride asked as he reached him.

"Mr. Walters didn't stay put. He's here. So's your pretty little psychic friend and some other woman."

McBride uttered a succinct oath. "Where are they?"

"I took 'em to the office." Theo led the way, two stairs at a time, but McBride's longer legs propelled him ahead as they reached the detective division at the end of the hall.

Andrew Walters sat in one of the chairs in front of McBride's desk, talking to a woman McBride didn't recognize. Lily stood across the room, her head turned toward the windows. Late afternoon sunlight bathed her face with golden light, causing McBride to falter before he caught himself and continued into the room.

Walters met him halfway, his expression tense. "Well?"

"Phony, like you thought. There were newspaper clippings about Abby's kidnapping all over his house, but no sign that she'd ever been around. He's being booked."

"Can I see him?" Walters asked.

McBride passed his hand over his face, suddenly tired. "I guess so. Our guys will want to interrogate him first."

"Can I watch?"

McBride motioned to Baker. "Theo, take Mr. Walters

with you to observe Biddle's interrogation." He crossed to his desk, pressing his hands to his weary eyes.

He expected Lily and the unknown woman to follow Theo and Walters out. But when he dropped his hands, the two women remained, Lily still standing by the window and the unidentified woman sitting primly in front of him, studying him with a pair of sparkling brown eyes.

"Who the hell are you?" he asked.

She laughed, and he saw the resemblance. He glanced at Lily. "She belongs to you?"

Lily's lips curved. "I don't usually claim her." She gave a little wave. "My sister Rose. Rose, this is Lieutenant J. McBride."

Rose held out her hand. "Nice to meet you. What's the J. stand for?"

McBride ignored her question and her extended hand, his eyes still on Lily. "I thought you were going to stay away from Walters."

Lily didn't answer.

"You're right, he *is* a grouch." Rose stood and looked down her nose at him, a twinkle in her light brown eyes. "I'll leave you to your spat in a minute, but I have just one more question. Are you married?"

McBride stared up at her, flummoxed. "No. Why?"

Rose just gave her sister a knowing look. Lily lowered her head, color flooding her neck and cheeks.

When Rose was gone, McBride looked across at Lily. "You could have asked me that yourself."

She lifted her chin and met his gaze. "I should have asked before. Considering."

He clenched his left hand into a fist, haunted by a phantom memory of cool gold circling his left ring finger. "I was married. My wife died a little over five years ago."

Lily crossed to him, her wild-honey eyes soft with concern. "I didn't know. I'm sorry."

He'd never figured out how to respond to those two words. Did he say thank-you? Or, it's not your fault? As usual, he said nothing.

She touched his cheek. "I wish I'd been wrong about the hoax, too. I wanted you to find Abby safe and sound."

He took a shaky breath, wanting nothing more than to press his face to her stomach and hold her close. Her touch made him feel wide open and raw. He hadn't felt so much—good or bad—in a long time. He'd thought it was better that way, feeling nothing. But he was beginning to realize feeling nothing was its own kind of pain.

He closed his eyes, overwhelmed by her warmth, by the slow, rhythmic stroke of her fingers on his face. He couldn't find the energy to sound stern when he asked, "Why are you here?"

"Andrew phoned and said you'd traced the call." She slid her hand down his neck to settle on his shoulder.

He opened his eyes. Her wary gaze met his and he realized she had her own walls to breach. Somehow the knowledge only made him feel more vulnerable.

She stroked his shoulder, her fingers brushing against his neck. He leaned into her caress, unable to resist the comfort she offered.

She moved behind him, pressing her soft hands against his skull, and began to rub his throbbing temples. When she drew his head back against her belly, he didn't resist. Her touch drove out the cold ache that had crept into his core when he'd arrived at Biddle's house and found no sign of Abby Walters. McBride hadn't realized until that moment just how much he'd been hoping he was wrong and that she would be there, alive and well, for him to rescue and return to her father.

"You must be exhausted." Her voice purred through him. "I know you couldn't have gotten much sleep on my sofa, and you've been on this case night and day."

"It'll be that way until all the leads are exhausted."

"Or until you find her."

He leaned his head back to look at her. "I wish I believed that."

"I know." She ran the back of her fingers down his cheek, her soft skin rasping on his day's growth of beard. "Rose is staying at my place tonight. Join us for dinner."

He smiled at the thought. "I suspect your sister is best experienced in small doses. I've had mine for today."

"Then tomorrow?" she pressed.

He tried to read her intentions behind those liquid gold eyes. "Dinner?"

"I'm not much of a cook, but I can come up with something."

He swiveled the desk chair, turning to face her. "Why?"

A flicker of fear passed across her face, and she took a half step back. But he read her answer in her wary eyes. He caught her hand, keeping her close.

"We could hurt each other in so many ways," he whispered.

Her lips trembled. "I know."

"We'd be crazy to even try it."

She nodded but took a step toward him, her legs sliding between his knees. She cupped his face between her palms. "Tomorrow night at seven?"

"Work is crazy. I can't promise to be on time."

"I'll keep dinner warm until you get there." She leaned in to kiss him.

The rattle of the doorknob gave them a second's notice before the door to the office began to open. Lily stepped away from him, robbing him of her warmth. She was on the other side of his desk by the time Theo, Walters and Rose walked in.

"He claims you got the wrong man." Walters's grim smile was chilling. "But he matches the description of the man in Lily's vision, so I know it's him."

McBride glanced at Lily. Her face was a porcelain mask, expressionless. "I'm sorry we didn't find her today," she said.

Walters looked at Lily. "We will."

McBride walked them down to the front lobby. While Rose led Walters ahead, Lily lingered behind. She lifted her face when they reached the front desk. "You could do with some rest, McBride."

He bent toward her, wishing they were in a less public place. "I'm glad you came here today."

For a split second bright light washed over her face, then was gone. It took another second for McBride to realize it had been the flash of a camera. He looked in the direction from which it had come.

A cluster of reporters were gathered around Walters and Lily's sister near the doorway. McBride strode over to the group, Lily on his heels. "Come on, guys, let Mr. Walters pass."

One of the reporters thrust his microphone toward Lily. "Ms. Browning, is it true that Mr. Walters has asked you to assist him in finding his daughter?"

Lily's face went pale, but she didn't answer. She tried

to move away, but the crowd hemmed her in, separating her from McBride.

"Are you a psychic, Ms. Browning? Do you claim to have had visions about the kidnapping?" the reporter pressed.

Andrew Walters caught Lily's arm, drawing her to his side. When he bent and said something in her ear, McBride felt his stomach coil into a hard knot. Old bitterness rose from deep inside, swamping him with doubt. Lily said she had only Abby's welfare at heart, but here she was, ready to work the cameras—

Only she wasn't. She was gazing at McBride, her eyes pleading, as if begging for rescue.

He pushed through the crowd and drew her out of the mass of reporters. "Ms. Browning has no comment." He bundled her through the front door, past the phalanx of newspeople.

Rose caught up with them at the bottom of the steps. "Wow, that was like a scene from a movie."

"Where's Walters?" McBride asked.

"He's giving the reporters a story. Said it might help him find Abby." Rose straightened her twisted blouse. "I think one of those reporters pinched my butt."

McBride glanced at Lily, a smile tugging at his lips. Her eyes met his, bright with amusement, and he let out a chuckle. A second later, Lily joined him.

Rose stared at them with mock outrage. "Yeah, well, it wasn't your butts."

McBride grinned broadly and held out his hand to her. "It's been nice meeting you, Rose Browning."

"Same here." She shook his hand firmly and headed toward the car, leaving him alone with Lily.

He turned and gazed into Lily's laughing eyes. "Anybody pinch your butt?"

She caught his hand, gave it a squeeze. "Sadly, no. Thanks for the rescue."

"Guess I was wrong. You're not a media hound, after all."

Her smile faded. She tried to let go of his hand, but he held on, keeping her close for a moment more.

"I'm sorry. I didn't mean to upset you." He caressed the back of her hand with his thumb. "I'll see you tomorrow night?"

Her smile returned. "Tomorrow night."

He let her go, and she began to walk away. When she reached the car, he spoke her name. "Lily?"

She turned to look at him. "Yeah?"

"Maybe we *will* find Abby safe and sound," he said.

She smiled slightly. "Maybe we will."

But it was a lie, he thought as he watched her get into her car and drive away. He had a sick feeling that if they ever found Abby Walters, safe and sound was the last thing she'd be.

Chapter Ten

The story made the Saturday morning newspaper: Psychic Joins Police In Search For Missing Child. Almost covering the top right corner of the paper, a candid photo captured Lily and McBride, heads close as they spoke. The caption implied she and McBride were conferring on the case.

Lily sank onto the sofa in dismay, paper in hand.

There were lots of quotes from Andrew Walters. Ever the politician, he knew how to turn the reporters' hostile questions into an asset. Though he never admitted that Lily was a psychic working to find his daughter, he made sure that the thrust of the article became a heartfelt plea for Abby's return.

Unfortunately, the journalist seemed to have done some background research on her, interviewing people from Willow Grove who'd known her when she was growing up. People whose names she barely recognized all had stories about those strange Browning girls and their odd ways. Worse, the article mentioned her job as a teacher at Westview Elementary. Now every reporter covering the case had her name and her occupation.

It wouldn't take long for them to hunt her down.

She was tempted to take Rose's advice and go home to Willow Grove for the rest of the weekend. But Lily needed to catch up on grading papers before Monday morning.

She saw her sister off after breakfast. "Call me to let me know you got home safely."

Rose gave her a hug. "Be safe yourself, Lil. Okay?"

After she left, Lily settled down with the stack of student papers Carmen Herrera had dropped off Friday. By noon, she'd worked her way through most of them and was considering taking a break for lunch when her spine started tingling.

Abby, she thought, relief mingling with the gray mist washing over her. She hadn't realized how much she'd needed to see the little girl again.

Seconds later, she was in Abby's tiny prison. The girl stood on her bed, peering out the small window. Lily strained to focus. "What're you looking at, Abby?"

The little girl whirled around. "Lily?"

"It's me, sweetie. Is there something out there?"

Abby turned back to the window. "I saw the mean man leave awhile ago, but he's back now."

"The mean man?"

Abby nodded. "He yells at me. The other one's nicer. His name's Gordy. The mean one's called Skeet. He hits me." She looked indignant. "Mama says you're not s'posed to hit people."

Lily wished she could put her arms around the little girl and never let her go. "Do they ever say where you are? Do they mention place names or street names?"

Abby's face crumpled. "I don't know. I'm sorry, Lily."

Her heart twisted. "It's okay, baby. You just try to listen and remember everything Gordy and Skeet say, okay? Then you tell me all about it. It'll be our little game."

"Can she play, too?" Abby asked.

The skin on the back of Lily's neck prickled. "She?"

"She means me," a child's voice said.

Lily whirled around. The mysterious dark-haired child of her previous vision stood in the shadows near the door. Gina, Lily thought, remembering what the girl had told her. *Mama calls me Gina, but I don't think that's my name.*

Gina smiled at Lily, her expression a heartbreaking mix of fear and hope. "Can I play, too, Lily?"

"Of course." Shudders rippled down Lily's spine.

The dark-haired girl sat on the edge of Abby's bed. "Abby can't see you like I can, Lily. Why not?"

"You can see her?" Abby's eyes were wide.

"Yeah. I can see you, too. But you can't see us."

"Why not?" Abby asked.

"I don't know," Lily admitted.

"I told Abby you have dark hair and gold eyes and you look like a fairy princess." The little girl sat next to Abby. The bed didn't shift physically, Lily noted with curiosity. Gina definitely wasn't there in the room with Abby.

"Gina, how often do you visit Abby?"

"My name's Casey," she replied with a frown.

"Why do you think that's your name?" Lily asked.

"Daddy talks to me in my dreams. He calls me Casey. He's going to teach me how to play bestball." Casey's heart-shaped face screwed up in a serious frown. "What's bestball?"

"I think you mean baseball." Lily wondered how a

child Casey's age could live in America and not know about baseball. "It's a game you play with a stick and a ball. Casey, do you ever hear the men who are holding Abby?"

"No. You want me to try? Is that how to play the game?"

Lily stared at her, overwhelmed by the strangeness of her presence in the vision. Where did Casey come from? Was she a real child or something else? A ghost? Abby's guardian angel? Lily grasped for an explanation that didn't include committing herself to an asylum.

Not a guardian angel, she decided. Gina—Casey—had her own troubles, including a mother who called her the wrong name.

But her daddy called her Casey.

The mists tugged at Lily, pulling her toward the real world. Her struggle was brief, the slightest resistance causing pain to shoot through her skull. "I'll be back," she promised the children as the gray fog swallowed her. Abby faded right away, but Casey lingered, a forlorn watcher in the mist.

Lily came back to herself slowly, her sluggish mind trying to make sense of the pale, geometric patterns on the ceiling above her. Sunlight reflected through the blinds on her living room windows, she realized after a moment. She was on the sofa. She'd been grading papers when the vision hit….

"Back among the living now?"

Lily jumped at the rumbling sound of McBride's voice.

He sat a few feet away in a boxy armchair too small for his frame, legs stretched out in front of him. His arms draped over the sides of the chair, fingers almost brushing the floor. His chin rested against his chest as if he was napping, but his eyes were open.

Watching her.

Her heart hammered in her chest.

He sat up, arms sliding forward to rest on his thighs. His gaze never left her. "I knocked. You didn't answer."

She cleared her throat. "What time is it?"

"Noon." McBride rubbed his jaw, his palm making a whispery scraping sound against his cheek. "Guess you saw the paper."

She rubbed her own face. "Yeah."

"You just had a vision," he said flatly.

She swallowed hard. "Yes."

He said nothing else, his gaze narrowed.

Then Lily remembered something Abby had told her. "Their names! Abby told me the names they use. Skeet and Gordy."

He sat back, his eyes wary. "Abby told you."

Her heart sank at his reaction. "At least check it out."

"I will." He rose from the chair, moving toward the door.

Lily intercepted him, closing her fingers around his arm. "Please don't do this."

He didn't pretend not to know what she was talking about. "I told you this would be a problem for us."

"You also told me to come to you with what I see."

"I'm not talking about the case. I'm talking about this." He laced his fingers through hers, pulling her closer.

"You don't believe. I knew that going in."

"How long before you resent me for it?" He lifted his hand to her cheek, his fingers sliding along the curve of her jaw. He bent close, his breath whispering across her lips. "How long before this isn't enough?"

McBride's mouth slanted across hers, hard and hungry. She slipped her hands up his back, tracing the contours of his spine, the flare of his shoulder blades. She smoothed her hands down his rib cage, over the small of his back, down to the curve of his buttocks. Squeezing gently, she urged his hips into the welcoming softness of her belly.

His breath exploded into her mouth, his body's response unmistakable. His arms tightened around her, lifting her up and propelling her backward.

Her knees hit the edge of the sofa and she fell back, pulling McBride with her. He caught himself with his arms to keep from landing with his full weight atop her. She stared at him, her breath bursting from her lungs in short gasps.

Time stood still.

Then he bent his head again, closing his lips over hers.

This kiss was different from any they'd shared before. It was slower, more thorough. Lingering, nipping, suckling. He brushed her chin, her cheeks with his lips, planted soft, sweet kisses on her eyelids and the tip of her nose. Her heart swelled, snared in the flood of passion sweeping over them.

McBride closed his hand over her breast, his palm circling gently, stroking her through her T-shirt. She moaned as her nipple tightened in response.

He rose over her, gazing down at her as if to memorize every freckle, every eyelash, every tiny line of her face. In his desire-darkened eyes, she saw her own reflection, the tangled hair and passion-drunk eyes of a woman falling in love.

He lowered his mouth to hers, slowly, tenderly. Her lips softened. Heat spread through her in great, velvety waves.

Suddenly, something hit McBride from behind with surprising force, and he drew away from her, uttering a loud oath. Lily blinked with surprise and found herself looking up at two sets of eyes—McBride's and Jezebel's.

He rolled away from her, the cat clinging to his shoulder. Lily scrambled to her knees and reached for the feline. "Jezzy, no!"

Jezebel clung for another moment, then released her death grip and bounded away. McBride reached over his shoulder, his fingers probing the small tears the cat's claws had left in his cotton dress shirt.

Lily gazed at the torn cloth with horror. "I'm so sorry, I don't know what came over her. She never acts that way."

He rubbed his shoulder, looking more frustrated than angry. "Probably thought I was trying to hurt you."

She put her hands on his shoulders, turning him so that she could check his wounds. "Cats aren't like Lassie. They figure we can take care of ourselves." Her lips curved. "But they are territorial. She's usually the one on top of me."

McBride looked toward the windowsill, where Jezebel sat like an Egyptian statue, turquoise eyes glaring at him. "Sorry."

Lily laughed softly and rose from the sofa. "I have some antibiotic ointment in the bathroom."

By the time she got back, he had his shirt off. She'd known he was muscular, but the shirt had hidden just how well built he really was. He was leaner than she'd expected, his muscles well defined but not bulky.

She crossed to him, ointment in hand, wondering how she could possibly touch him again without throwing him back down on the sofa. Somehow she managed to apply the ointment to his scratches without letting her hands wander. "There."

He looked at her, his eyes dark with lingering passion. She touched his cheek, her heart squeezing as he rubbed his face against her palm and pressed his lips against the fleshy part of her thumb.

She cradled his head and bent to kiss him.

But he gently pulled away, rising from the sofa. "I realize it's a little late to remember this, but I'm still on duty." He lifted her hands to his lips, kissed her knuckles lightly and took a step away from her. "How are you going to get to work Monday?"

"I guess I need to rent a car." She should have done it while Rose was here to drive her around.

He shook his head. "I'll drive you to work Monday and we can see about renting a car that afternoon when I pick you up. What time do you need to be there?"

"I try to get there by six-thirty."

He grimaced but nodded. "I'll be here at six."

"Okay." Lily walked him to the front door, her body buzzing with unfulfilled need.

McBride nodded toward Jezebel, who still glared at them from the window ledge. His lips curved slightly. "I think she's still looking for an apology," he murmured, dropping a quick kiss on Lily's cheek before he left.

Closing the door behind him, Lily turned and glared at the animal. "Forget getting an apology from me, brat cat."

She should probably be grateful that Jezebel had stopped them before things went too far. With all the obstacles to their tenuous relationship, jumping into sex this quickly was probably a very bad idea.

But damn, it had felt like a good one at the time.

LILY HAD THOUGHT she'd be glad to be back at school. But as much as she'd missed her kids, she found it impossible to concentrate on work.

All she could think about was McBride.

They had come so close to making love Saturday. The memory of his mouth on hers was so vivid it made her body grow warm and liquid with need.

But that had happened two days ago, and since that time she'd had a chance to think long and hard about what was going on between them.

The truth was, she and McBride were wrong for each other. There wasn't a chance in hell they'd ever form a lasting relationship together.

Because she was a psychic.

There. She'd admitted it.

She was a psychic. She'd spent most of her life hating the word, hating the idea, but the truth was she couldn't change what she was, no matter how much she wanted to.

And for the first time, she didn't think she wanted to.

She had a gift, just like her sisters. Like most gifts, it came with strings attached. What she saw in her visions often brought her pain. There would be many visions she'd rather escape. But if her recent visions of Abby had done nothing else, they'd taught her that sometimes her gift could be a blessing as well as a curse.

She'd helped Abby. She'd comforted the child, helped her not be so afraid. God willing, her visions would lead her to Abby soon. Lily could never turn her back on her gift now.

Not even for McBride.

She sensed that something dark and horrible had happened to the detective. Something that made belief impossible for him.

So she had a decision to make. She could either take what she could get, knowing that it wouldn't end well, or stop playing with fire now before she got burned.

Which was it going to be?

By the time the school bell rang at three, she was no closer to an answer. And McBride would be there soon, forcing her hand. She tried to distract herself by getting a head start on grading the day's papers while she waited.

But by ten to four, McBride still hadn't shown.

Carmen stuck her head through the doorway just after four, her expression full of curiosity. "Got a call from Lieutenant McBride. He's stuck in traffic, but he's on his way. You want to call him, tell him I'll give you a ride?"

Lily knew she should probably take Carmen up on the offer, but realized that by avoiding McBride, she'd be only delaying her decision. "I'll be fine. I'm sure he'll be here soon."

"Okay. Everybody else has left, but Roy's in the gym sweeping up, and Mabel is over at the portable classrooms if you need anything." Carmen left with a little wave.

Lily passed the time preparing her own classroom for the next day's lessons. The air was thick with silence, the deep hush that could be found only in places like schools, as if the remembered sounds of children laughing and talking somehow made the rare quiet tangible.

When the classrooms emptied, the thermostat had been turned down. Lily shivered and pulled her warm cardigan more tightly around her, looking out the window toward the school entrance. She wished McBride would hurry.

She was about to turn away from the window when she saw a car pull into the parking lot. She thought it was him for a moment, until she realized the vehicle was the wrong make. It disappeared beyond the building.

The hair on the back of her neck rose.

She dipped her hand into her purse and pulled out her keys. A small vial of pepper spray was attached to the key chain; she unsnapped the safety tab from the vial and slipped into the dark, deserted hallway.

Her footfalls sounded like thunder in the void, rivaled only by the roar of her pulse in her ears. She forced herself to take deep, steady breaths as she walked quickly to the second-grade classroom that faced the faculty parking lot. She slipped through the door and hurried to the window.

The car was a light-colored sedan, maybe a Ford. The driver's door opened and a man stepped out, a baseball cap low over his face. Lily backpedaled slowly, watching the man move furtively toward the side door, disappearing from sight.

Her heart racing, she wondered if the door was locked, and decided she didn't have time to make sure it was. She whirled and ran from the room, heading for the front entrance. There were homes across the street; if she could get there safely, she could knock on doors until she found someone to help her.

She hit the front door running, but it didn't open. She pushed again, rattled the metal panel, but it was locked. So was its mate.

She banged her hand against the second door with frustration. The sound echoed through the empty hall and died away, supplanted by her ragged breathing.

And a furtive noise down the hall.

Lily held her breath.

There it was again. A soft scraping noise, metal on metal. A soft, hollow rattle.

He was opening a window.

Okay, don't panic. There has to be another way out.

The gymnasium. Of course.

Carmen had said Roy was there, cleaning. The gym was on the far side of the building, and the sounds she was hearing indicated the intruder was somewhere between.

But there was more than one way to the gym. And she had the advantage of familiarity.

Lily sped silently toward the lunchroom doors halfway down the hall. She could no longer hear the window rattling, but surely he hadn't had time to crawl through yet.

She covered the last few yards and was reaching for the door handle when she saw him. All in black, from dusty boots to the knit ski mask he must have donned on his way in, he filled a doorway ten yards to her left.

He froze, surprise evident in his stiff posture. She went still as well, just for a second.

Then she bolted through the cafeteria door.

The door swung shut behind her, hitting him with a soft thud as he followed her. She kept her back to the cafeteria wall as she scooted across the room, knowing his eyes wouldn't adjust to the dark for a few seconds. He'd probably waste time feeling for a light switch that wasn't there, not knowing it was on the side of the room where the faculty sat, so that mischievous students couldn't play games with the lights.

She was almost to the end of the cafeteria before she heard him closing in behind her. She sped up, knees knocking into chairs as she skimmed past tables in her frantic dash for the door.

Her fingers brushed the cool metal handle but missed. She groped again, but it was too late. Arms like tree trunks crushed her, squeezing the air from her lungs.

"Where you goin', Lily?" His breath burned her ear. She smelled stale cigarettes and peppermint. The combination almost made her gag. She didn't recognize the voice, so it wasn't the one Abby called Skeet. The mean one.

Lily clutched the little vial of pepper spray in her hand, wondering if she could get far enough away from him to use the spray without also incapacitating herself.

"What do you want?" She could barely gasp out the words.

His grip tightened, constricting her air further. He lifted her half off her feet, jerking her toward the door. "I was gonna leave a little note for you in your classroom, but since you're here, I'll deliver it in person."

He whirled her around and pinned her to the wall. Her elbows banged against the porcelain tile, pain shooting down to her fingertips and threatening her grip on the pepper spray. But she gritted her teeth and held on.

"Stay away from this thing." He spoke slowly. Clearly. "I know the feds are watching your house. They've tapped your phone by now, haven't they? Do you really want the headache of being involved in this case?"

She wrinkled her nose at the sour smell of his breath. Fear still pulsed through her veins, but anger was catching up.

I know something, too, she thought, lifting her chin. "You don't know as much as you think you do. Like, at this very minute, there's a policeman on his way here to take me home."

"Don't try to bluff me, Lily."

"Didn't you notice my car wasn't in the lot?"

He jerked her to her toes and slammed her back against the wall. "Your car was totaled the other night."

Her heart caught. "You drove me off the road."

"And you still didn't get the message, did you?" He tightened his grip on her. "So I'll deliver it face-to-face. Stay away from this case. Tell Walters you're through. Tell that cop you want out. Got it?"

She bit back the pain radiating from her bruised spine. "What are you afraid of? That I know who you are?"

He let her go suddenly, as if her skin had sent out an electrical pulse. Taking advantage of her momentary freedom, Lily lifted her hand in a smooth arc and pressed the top of the pepper spray dispenser. A noxious cloud of stinging spray filled the air, some of it floating back toward her even as she ducked and ran.

Her eyes stung and began to tear up, but she didn't slow down, weaving through the maze of tables and chairs toward the lunchroom door. She heard coughing and cursing behind her, closer than she liked. The ski mask the man was wearing must have blocked some of the spray.

She hit the lunchroom door with a thud and burst through, darting to the left.

With a crunch of shattering glass, her attacker slammed through the door behind her, too close.

Lily turned the corner and ducked into the male faculty bathroom, locking it. She retreated to the back stall and crouched in the corner, her breath coming in harsh rasps.

She'd just run herself into a trap.

Chapter Eleven

McBride pulled into the paved circle in front of the school, cursing himself for taking the expressway. He was almost an hour late, after making such a big deal over driving Lily to school for her own safety. If she'd rented a car on Saturday as she had suggested, she'd be safe at home instead of sitting alone in an almost empty school, waiting for him to arrive. She was probably ticked off at him, with good reason.

He headed up the walkway to the front door and pulled the handle. The door rattled but didn't open.

Locked.

He frowned. Had she found a ride home?

He walked around the building toward a cluster of portable classrooms, where a tall, handsome black woman was locking up. She gave a start as she turned to see him.

"Sorry. I'm looking for Ms. Browning to give her a ride home, but the front door is locked."

The black woman smiled. "Oh, Ms. Herrera always locks that door when she leaves. Roy and me—Roy's my husband—we clean up after hours and go out the back doors when we leave. Ms. Herrera told me Lily was waiting on somebody. Says you're a policeman." She peered at him. "Mind if I see your badge?"

He smiled and showed her his shield.

She pulled a set of keys from a ring on her belt, led him around to the front and unlocked the door. "Lily's room is that way." She pointed. "Fourth one on the left. Y'all come get me when you leave, and I'll lock it up." She headed back around the building.

McBride hurried down the hall to Lily's classroom. He stepped through the door, already opening his mouth to apologize. But the room was empty.

"Lily?" He took a quick look around to make sure he wasn't missing a hidden closet or cloakroom. He saw her purse lying open on top of her desk. But no Lily.

He stepped back into the hall and looked down the darkened corridor. He was about to call her name when he heard a muted scraping sound. He went still, instinct taking over. Easing the 9mm Smith & Wesson from his holster, he held his breath, listening carefully.

He heard another soft rattle, then a brittle banging noise, like something hitting a window. His stomach clenched with tension and the beginnings of fear as he crept toward the noise.

The sounds were coming from a room two doors down.

By the time he reached the doorway, he hadn't heard any sounds for several seconds. He readied himself just outside the door, straining to hear any noise, however tiny. He looked down to ground himself, sucking in a deep preparatory breath.

And saw the splatters of blood.

Blackness poured into his brain. He fought through the fear and braced himself, running through police procedure like a mantra. *Go in low, cover your back, stay alert.*

He had to do it. He had to do it now.

He burst into the room, pistol held firmly in the correct two-hand grip. He swept the room with the gun and his sharp eyes, quickly ascertaining that it was empty.

At least, it was empty now.

He crossed to the open window, careful to remain low. He saw movement outside, a blur of cream. A car, he realized, speeding out of the parking lot too fast for him to get more than a cursory look at the make and model, much less anything like a license plate. It careened down the street, ran a stop sign without even slowing and disappeared from sight.

McBride holstered his gun and turned away from the window. He had already taken a couple of steps toward the door when he noticed the smell.

Pepper spray, sharp and burning in his nostrils.

For the first time, he saw the dark lump on the floor. He fished a pen from his pocket and lifted the object. The acrid pepper odor intensified.

It was a black knit ski mask.

Acid spewed into McBride's stomach. He dropped the mask and ran to the door. "Lily!"

The sound echoed down the empty corridor.

"Lily!" He peered through the gloom at the spatters of blood, trying to follow their trail. They weaved down the hall in widely spaced droplets. Whoever had been bleeding had ducked into each room, as if searching for something.

Or someone.

McBride followed the trail around a corner to the men's

bathroom. Several drops of blood marred the tile floor in front of the door, as if the injured person had stood there for several seconds. The next drop of blood was about five feet down the hall.

The trail of blood ended at the door of the cafeteria. The glass window set in the door was broken. McBride found a torn fragment of black fabric on one of the jagged shards of glass still in the window.

He bent closer, trying not to disturb the shattered glass on the floor. The fragment looked like leather—from a glove?

Panic buzzed down his spine. He pushed the fear away and forced himself to focus. There'd been an intruder. There was blood—probably from the perp, he reassured himself, looking at the broken glass.

But where was Lily?

There was no way the intruder could've gotten through that window with Lily. If she were conscious, she'd have been kicking and screaming. And if she were unconscious, she'd be too unwieldy to pull through such a small space.

She had to be here somewhere.

He retraced his steps, following the blood spatter. At the door to the men's bathroom, he again noted the extra blood outside the door. He gave the door a push.

It didn't budge.

"Lily?"

A jingling noise startled him. He whipped his gun up.

A tall, thin black man dropped his key ring to the floor with a clatter and lifted his hands, his eyes wide with shock.

McBride lowered his weapon and flashed his shield. "Police. Got a key to this bathroom?"

LILY HAD BARELY registered the sound of McBride's voice outside the bathroom when the door in her mind exploded open, sucking her through the portal into raw fear edged with the coldest, blackest darkness she'd ever known. Emotions battered her—terror, despair, guilt, grief, hate. Darkness filled her lungs and seeped into her skin, covering her, drowning her.

A woman's voice inhabited her mind so completely that the words she muttered seemed to be her own. "She's gone, McBride. Clare's gone. I can't find her. Clare!"

Lily sobbed with anguish. "Oh, Clare, my baby!"

She felt hands on her shoulders, hot against her freezing flesh, dragging her from the whirlpool of grief. Eyes opening, she saw McBride's face close to hers. She clung to him as he drew her out of her dark vision, gasping for air as the blackness released her from its grasp.

But the anguish remained, pouring out in a tormented cry. "She's gone, McBride. Clare's gone!"

MCBRIDE RELEASED Lily's arms and staggered backward into the bathroom wall. The room swam as he stared into her vacant eyes, his ears ringing with her anguished words.

She's gone, McBride. Clare's gone!

The voice had been Lily's, but the tone, the inflection, the anguish had been Laura's. Grief had etched his late wife's words into his soul. There could be no mistake.

He barely heard the janitor's voice. "Good Lord, Lily!"

A few feet away, Lily bent over the urinal, retching and crying. The janitor hovered over her, waving his hands ineffectually, apparently unsure what to do.

Battering down grief to the dark place inside him,

McBride walked to the sink, wet several paper towels and took them to Lily, who hung over the urinal, fighting dry heaves.

He crouched next to her and bathed her flushed face.

"It was the man who ran me off the road," she said.

McBride sat back on his heels. "Are you sure?"

"He said I didn't get the message that time, so he decided to deliver it face-to-face. Did you see him?"

"Just a glimpse of his car." He brushed her sweat-dampened hair away from her cheeks, looking for injuries. "Did he hurt you? There was blood—"

"I think he put his hand through the lunchroom door."

DNA, McBride thought, trying to focus on his job. He'd get the crime scene unit to gather samples. "He left his mask behind. Did you hit him with pepper spray?"

She nodded.

He gently wiped her mouth. "Did he say why he was here?"

"He wants me to stay away from the case." She shivered.

McBride slipped his arm around her to warm her, although he felt so cold inside he wasn't sure it would do much good. He helped her stand and led her out of the bathroom into the dark hallway.

She wrapped her arms more tightly around her trembling body. "I'm sorry I'm not much help," she murmured.

Torn between wanting to hold her and wanting to run as far away from her as he could get, McBride compromised by doing neither—and doing his job. "Did you get a look at him?"

"Before he entered the building. He's tall, about your size." Her teeth chattered. "He already had the mask on, so I didn't see his face or his coloring, except he was Caucasian. I wasn't close enough to see the color of his eyes except when he caught me in the cafeteria, and then it was too dark."

"He caught you?" The thought of the masked man touching her sent rage flooding through him.

She rubbed her upper arms. "I was running from him. He grabbed me and pinned me against the wall."

McBride reached for her. She wrapped her arms around his waist and pressed her face to his throat.

The janitor cleared his throat. "I'm gonna check and see if Mabel's all right. We'll call the police."

"Ask for Captain Vann in the detective bureau," McBride said. "Say McBride told you to call and that it's connected to the Walters kidnapping."

The janitor's eyes widened. "I'll do that."

McBride cradled Lily's face between his hands, searching her pale face. "Are you sure you're all right?"

She nodded. "I'm just a little shaky."

He had a feeling Lily wasn't shaken nearly as much by the intruder as by whatever the hell had happened in that bathroom, when she'd cried to him in Laura's grief-stricken words.

Had she really seen that horrible scene from his past?

No. It could have been a calculated guess. That was the game the phonies played, wasn't it? Take a few facts, make some savvy guesses and play it up big time.

He'd seen it before.

But how could Lily have known about Clare? From newspaper archives? Could she have pieced things together, made some smart guesses and created a scenario to match past reality?

No. Lily wasn't that cruel. She wasn't playing games.

But if she wasn't, then she was telling the truth about her visions. Something McBride wasn't ready to believe.

THE BLUE GLOW OF streetlamps poured through the windows of McBride's office, holding back the darkness but not the late autumn chill. Shivering, Lily leaned back from McBride's desk and rubbed her burning eyes. He was in the captain's office across the hall, conferring with his task force. He'd apologized for not being able to take her straight home. "We have to go over everything that's happened today."

She'd waved off his apology. "Go."

Now she was beginning to miss him. She was safe enough—who would come after her in a station full of armed cops?—but the silence was starting to get to her.

So it was with relief that she heard the door across the hallway open and footsteps move toward McBride's office. McBride entered the room, closing the door behind him. "You holding up?"

She nodded, wishing he would touch her. She needed to feel his hand on her skin, reassuring her that everything was all right.

He crouched beside her, placing his hands on her knees. She shivered, her body leaping in response to his light touch. "Let's get you home."

"Agent Brody wanted to talk to me, didn't he?" She wished McBride would kiss her. The heat of his mouth over hers would chase away the chill that had settled into her bones.

"I told Brody it could wait." He touched his lips to her forehead, then pulled her out of the chair and into his arms.

Bending his head, he kissed her lightly. "We'll stop by my place so I can get some clothes, and then I'll take you home."

She looked up, trying to read his expression. Though his kiss had been sweet, she'd detected a hint of distance in his posture. No big surprise; he'd been shaken by what had happened today. By her ordeal, certainly, but also by what had occurred when he'd found her in the bathroom.

She would never forget the look on his face when she'd surfaced from her hellish vision with another woman's words on her lips. For a moment, he'd seemed like a dead man, eyes empty, soul vacant. He had recognized the words, the pain.

Tomorrow, she decided, she'd make him tell her about Clare.

McBRIDE SLEPT WITH LILY that night. Just slept, neither of them thinking about passion after the day's ordeal. McBride woke every few hours, unable to sleep for very long before being awakened by dark, twisted nightmares he didn't dare remember in the light. Each time, he found Lily sleeping peacefully beside him, her cats curled behind her like living bed warmers.

When he woke for good around 6:00 a.m., Lily was awake, sitting next to him with the cats in her lap. She greeted him with a sleepy smile. He sat up, rubbing his eyes. "What're you doing up so early?"

"I still work for a living."

He shook his head. "You're not going back there today."

"I have to go back sometime."

"Not today. You're exhausted."

"I'm fine." She cocked her head. "You look wiped, though."

He grinned. "I always look this bad."

"Not *always*," she murmured with a slight arch of her eyebrows and a devilish grin. "Sometimes you're almost okay-looking. I live for those moments."

He grinned at her. "Sweet-talker." He started to lean toward her when his cell phone shrilled. Groaning, he grabbed it from the night table. "McBride."

It was Captain Vann. "Just got a call from Walker County. They've got a juvenile Jane Doe, red hair, blue eyes, about five or six years old."

McBride's stomach sank. "How fresh?"

"Under twelve hours, they think."

Abby Walters, he thought immediately.

"They're e-mailing us the morgue photos in about half an hour," Vann said. "I'd like the whole task force here, just in case."

"I'll be there in fifteen minutes." McBride hung up the phone and looked at Lily. She gazed at him, her brow wrinkled with concern. He tried to keep his expression neutral, but she saw through him.

Her face went white. "Abby?"

McBride sat beside her and took her hand. Her fingers were icy. "Walker County cops have found a juvenile Jane Doe. They're e-mailing photos in a little while. The captain wants the task force present."

She shook her head mutely.

"It might not be her," he said, wishing he believed it.

She nodded but didn't look convinced. "Go on. I'll get one of the FBI agents outside to drive me to work."

McBride stroked her hand. "You can't go back to

school today. You'll just bring the press flocking there, disrupting the students."

She sighed in frustration, but he could see her accepting the inevitable. "Okay. I'll call Carmen."

Lily walked McBride to the door. "Phone me when you know something."

He kissed her brow. "I will. Try not to borrow trouble."

As he was getting into his car, his cell phone rang. It was Special Agent Cal Brody. His voice was grim. "I just got the message. Think it's her?"

"I hope to God not." McBride cranked the engine, steeling himself for what was about to come.

THE PHOTOS LOADED SLOWLY on the computer screen, revealing pixel by pixel the harsh face of death. Though he sat in the middle of a climate-controlled police station, McBride could feel the cold air of the morgue in the images, felt it seep under his jacket, spreading chill bumps across his flesh. He studied the pictures, forced himself to be thorough, before he turned away from the screen. "It's not her."

He got up and paced across the room, breathing deeply to drive out the imagined odor of death. He leaned against the door frame, longing for a double bourbon straight up, though he hadn't had a drink in years.

Special Agent Brody joined him. "Got a cigarette?"

"Don't smoke."

Brody's grin was horrible. "Neither do I."

McBride rubbed his face, unable to escape the image of that tiny white body lying on the metal slab. "You have any clue who that little girl could be?"

Brody shook his head. "Maybe she hasn't been

reported missing yet. The M.E. says it looks like she was raped and strangled."

McBride closed his eyes. Sharp, dark pain ate at his gut.

"Did Walters know about this call?"

"No."

"Good." McBride crossed the room to Theo's desk. His colleague looked up at him, silent compassion warming his dark brown eyes. "Theo, give Walker County a call and let them know that's not our girl."

He gave a nod and picked up the phone.

"I've got some new stuff on Paul Leonardi." Brody followed McBride back to his office. "Looks like his alibi is solid. We've tracked down people at every place he gave us, and between their register receipts and their personal memories, everything checks out."

"Damn." McBride dropped into his chair.

"What about the woman?" Brody added.

McBride slanted a look at the FBI agent. Brody's expression was hard to read, but he already knew the man shared his skepticism about all things paranormal. "I don't think she knows anything we can use."

"I meant, what about her as a suspect?"

McBride picked up the bottle of antacids on his desk, shaking a couple straight into his mouth. "She didn't call herself. She didn't drive herself off the road, and she didn't attack herself at the school yesterday."

"She could have an accomplice."

McBride couldn't argue. Lily's part in this whole mess was the one thing he couldn't make sense of. How was she involved? If she wasn't in on the kidnapping, why were people trying to hurt her? Because they believed she really was a psychic and were afraid she'd figure out who they were?

He rubbed his aching temples. "Nothing about her adds up."

"I'm just saying, it's awfully damn convenient that she seems to be right where the action is, every time." Brody gave him a hard look before going to talk to Captain Vann.

As the rest of the task force dispersed to their planned duties for the day, McBride picked up the phone and called Lily. She answered on the first ring. "It's not her," he said.

He heard her soft exhalation of relief. But a moment later, she said, "But it was somebody."

"Listen, I'm going to have to be here awhile longer. I'll call you later." He hung up, running a hand over his eyes.

Just hearing her voice tempted him to race back to her house and her waiting arms, but Brody was right. Lily was the big unanswered question sitting right in the middle of his investigation, and until he made sense of her part in the case, he had a feeling they'd never find out what had really happened to Abby Walters.

McBride grabbed Brody as he was about to head out. "You going to see Walters?"

"Yeah."

"I'll drive." Resolutely putting Lily out of his mind, McBride followed the FBI agent out of the office.

Chapter Twelve

"I'm sorry—I've been listening to the tape over and over, but I just don't recognize the voice," Walters said. "What does Lily say?"

McBride glanced at Brody. The agent's eyebrows twitched upward as McBride struggled for an answer that wouldn't sound crazy. "She thinks the caller was on the up and up."

"Did she recognize the voice?" Walters pressed.

McBride sighed, out of wiggle room. "Yeah, the voice on the phone. Not the one at the school, though."

Walters looked from McBride to Brody and back. "At the school? Someone contacted her at the school?"

Ignoring Brody's frown, McBride told Andrew Walters about the intruder at the school. "She's fine, just a little shaken."

"Thank God." Walters looked shaken himself. "I don't think I could live with myself if something happened to her because of what I've asked her to do."

Reassuring Walters that Lily was fine, McBride steered the interview back to the tape. "Maybe the kidnapper's connected to you somehow. Maybe a supporter you met at a rally."

"More likely a supporter of my opponent," Walters said blackly. "I knew he liked to play dirty, but—"

"Are you suggesting Senator Blackledge is connected to your daughter's kidnapping?" Brody's voice was quiet and grim.

Walters sighed. "I didn't say that."

Some of the task force had been dogging Gerald Blackledge for days as the savvy old senator beat the bushes in search of more votes. But given the way Walters was surging in the polls thanks to the sympathy vote, McBride couldn't see how kidnapping Abby would serve Blackledge's purposes. If he'd hoped that Walters would quit the race, he'd miscalculated badly.

Walters's cell phone rang. He glanced at the display panel. "I've got to get that."

"We'll see ourselves out," McBride said.

In the elevator down to the lobby, Brody gave McBride a measuring look. "I get Walters buying into the psychic business—but you don't, do you?"

"Of course not," McBride answered. But guilt nagged at him, giving his gut a nasty little tweak, as if he was being disloyal to Lily for scoffing at her visions.

He and Brody were back at the station by eleven-thirty. On his way to his office, he checked in with Alex Vann to tell him about the interview with Walters regarding the tape from Lily's answering machine. "Walters says he doesn't recognize the voice and he has no idea what the man means about finding a way to contact him."

As McBride headed out the door, Vann pushed up out

of his chair. "McBride, wait, there's something you need to know—"

McBride stopped short at the open door, his eyes widening when he saw the woman standing in the doorway across the hall. Her shiny blond hair glistened like silver in the glow of the overhead fluorescent lights.

His gut twisted. "Delaine."

THE FBI AGENT Lily convinced to drive her to the rental car place was happy for the change of scenery; surveillance was a pain in the ass, he'd confessed on the drive to the rental place. And he took a great deal of pleasure shaking the handful of reporters who'd mobbed them as they made their escape.

She'd picked out her clothing with care, settling on a pair of slim-fitting olive-green wool pants and a figure-hugging sage cashmere sweater. By the time she'd chosen just the right suede sling-back pumps to complete the look, she'd started thinking of the outfit as her coat of armor. Because once she picked up a rental car, she was on her way to McBride's office to slay a dragon.

Today, she was going to ask him about Clare. And she wasn't going to leave his office until he told her.

She picked another Buick, similar to her totaled car, needing that sense of familiarity. She gave in to Agent Logan's demand that he follow her to the police station, but shooed him away when he tried to stay until she'd finished her business inside.

"Lieutenant McBride will see me home," she promised. Logan looked reluctant, but did as she asked.

She was halfway up the stairs to McBride's office when her cell phone rang. Torn between impatience to get the coming confrontation over with and relief to have the inevitable fireworks postponed, Lily hesitated only a moment before answering.

It was Andrew Walters. "Lily, thank God you're all right! Lieutenant McBride told me what happened to you."

"I'm fine," she assured him.

"I think you should do what the man said. I don't want to be responsible for something bad happening to you."

Lily frowned. "You don't want me to help you anymore?"

"You could have been killed." Andrew's voice was a curious mixture of anxiety and persuasiveness.

No wonder he's a politician, she thought.

"The police haven't had any luck finding anyone with the names you gave them, and the scenes you've described from your visions are too vague to help them pinpoint her location."

She tried not to take his words as a rebuke of her abilities. She knew what she was seeing was real. In time, she'd come up with the clue to help them find Abby.

If they had time.

Andrew's voice grew gentle. "I don't want you hurt."

There was nothing threatening in the tone of Andrew's voice. But the hair on the back of her neck rose, anyway.

"I'll think about it," she agreed.

"Good." He rang off quickly, as if he'd accomplished what he'd set out to do. She hung up the phone more slowly, considering Andrew's request.

Could she turn her back on Abby just because things were getting a little dangerous for Lily herself?

MCBRIDE STARED AT Delaine Howard, fighting the urge to run. He'd never expected to see her again. God knew he didn't want to, especially on a day like today. But Delaine had always seemed to know when he was at his weakest.

He looked around the office to see if any other cops were there to run interference. But the rest of the day shift appeared to be out on calls. He closed the distance between them, noting with dark satisfaction the anxiety in her eyes. "What do you want?"

"I'm here about the kidnapping."

McBride thought the acid in his stomach was finally going to burn a hole all the way through. He moved past her and entered his office, grabbing the bottle of antacids from his desk. He crunched a couple between his teeth. "I suppose you've had a vision?"

"No." She paused in the doorway to his office. "I know you could never trust my visions again. Not after—"

"Cut the crap, Delaine. What do you want?"

She licked her lips and crossed to stand in front of his desk. "The woman on the news—Lily Browning—you have to listen to her. She can help you find that little girl. She has a powerful gift."

His gut rebelled. "I don't work with psychics."

Delaine frowned. "But the news said—"

"It's Andrew Walters's idea. He's a father whose little girl is missing." McBride impaled her with his hard glare. "People believe all kinds of crazy things when they're desperate."

A tear slid down her cheek. "I thought Clare would be where I told you."

"But she wasn't, was she?" McBride rose to his feet, bitter rage surging. "She wasn't anywhere you told us we could find her. Do you have any idea what you did to us? Laura's dead because of you! I might as well be. And *you* did that, Delaine. You kept our hopes alive until they destroyed us." His voice rang through the office, dying away into silence.

Then he realized he and Delaine were no longer alone.

Lily stood in the doorway, gazing at him with stricken eyes. "Clare was your daughter."

The sympathy in her voice was too much for him to bear. He backed away from her and held up his hands. "Don't."

Delaine caught Lily's arm. "Give him a minute."

Lily jerked her arm away. "Don't tell me what to do." She turned to McBride. "I'm not her. I didn't do this to you."

McBride looked at Delaine. "You need to go now."

Tears filled Delaine's eyes. "I am sorry, McBride. You have to know that I never meant for things to go so wrong—" Her voice broke on a sob and she hurried out of the office.

McBride dropped heavily into his chair, trying to control his emotions before he did something rash. He looked at Lily. "You should go, too."

"No."

The look of understanding in her eyes nearly made him come undone. He balled his fists at his sides, afraid of losing himself completely to the blackness inside him if she stayed much longer. "You can't lead me to Abby Walters. I don't believe you. I never will. And no matter what you say, I don't think you can live with that in the long run."

She closed her eyes, pain drawing lines in her forehead.

"Look at me," he demanded.

She squeezed her eyes more tightly shut, shaking her head.

He lurched from his desk and grabbed her arms. "Look at me, damn it!"

Her eyes flew open, wide and afraid.

"This is what happens if you're wrong. This is what Andrew Walters will become when he finally learns the truth about Abby." McBride gave her a hard shake and let her go.

She backed away, eyes shiny with tears. "Andrew wants me off the case."

A sliver of surprise worked its way into the darkness inside him. He'd thought that Walters would cling to false hope to the bitter end. "Good. Then it's settled."

"I can't back away from this."

"That's your problem." Anger receded, sucking him back into an icy black abyss. He sank onto the edge of his desk. "As far as I'm concerned, it's over. I'm through."

She stared at him, dumbfounded.

"Go home, Lily."

"McBride, you can't just—"

He cut her off. "I'm done."

Her unflinching gaze held his for a long, painful moment. Then, suddenly, she looked away. Her lips began to tremble. She turned and hurried out the door.

He groped for his chair and sat, burying his head in his hands, giving in to the shakes he'd held off ever since Lily had walked through the door and into the middle of his nightmare.

He needed a drink. One shot of Jack Daniels after another, burning a path down his gullet until he forgot about the big, black hole in his heart.

He dragged himself to his feet and grabbed his coat. It was time to reacquaint himself with an old, reliable friend.

HER HEAD POUNDING with the force of another vision, Lily struggled to reach her vehicle. The last thing she wanted to do when McBride was in this state was go into a trance in the middle of his office.

Racing down the front steps of the police station, she managed to slide behind the wheel of her rental car before the vision sucked her through the door in her mind, into the mists. She didn't fight it, letting the flow of the vision soothe away the burgeoning ache in her head.

She emerged into an old-fashioned parlor sheltered from the midday sun by juniper bushes growing outside. A woman sat in a rocking chair near the hearth, holding out her hands as if warming them in front of a fire. But no fire was lit.

"You came." Hearing the small voice, Lily turned around to find Casey in the doorway, a smile carving dimples in her cheeks. "I called," the dark-haired girl said. "Did you hear me?"

"Is this where you live?"

The child nodded, her smile fading. "That's Mama." She gestured toward the woman. "She's in one of her moods."

Lily moved closer to the figure in the rocking chair. She was a thin, pale woman about ten years older than Lily. She looked as though she'd been pretty once, but illness had slackened her jaw and glazed her blue eyes.

"I had another mama, but she died. My daddy couldn't take care of me, so I came to live with her." Casey knelt in front of the woman, pressing her cheek against her knee. "She didn't used to be so sad." Casey stroked her outstretched arm, but the woman didn't react.

Chills raced down Lily's spine. Was Casey even there? Or was she a ghost, the remnant of a child long dead? Had the woman gone crazy from grief? Was she paying no attention to Casey because Casey wasn't really there?

"I'm not a ghost," Casey said. "You have to be dead to be a ghost, and I'm not dead." She turned her head and looked at Lily, the directness of her gaze unnerving. "Are you dead?"

"No."

Casey smiled. "It would be okay if you were. I like you anyway. You're not scary."

Lily touched the girl's cheek, wondering if Casey would be able to feel it. The child rubbed her cheek against Lily's palm, her little-girl flesh soft and warm. Lily caressed the solemn, heart-shaped face.

"Will you come play with me?" Casey took her hand. Lily squeezed the small fingers, marveling at how real they felt.

Casey led her down a narrow hall to a tiny room decorated in fading pink and white. "This is my room," she said proudly.

Lily looked around the tiny, cluttered space, her heart aching. It was grimy, despite obvious attempts by someone to keep it tidy. How long had this child lived with her mother's madness, trying to carve out some semblance of a normal life?

Lily sat on the bed by Casey, who picked up a book from a rickety bedside table. "My favorite book," she said.

Lily recognized the bright cover; she'd been reading the same book to her class for the past couple of weeks. *"Boots and Belinda,"* she murmured. "It's one of my favorite books, too."

She settled on the side of the bed and listened, her heart aching, as Casey carefully read the first chapter aloud. She read well, under the circumstances, though she mispronounced some of the more unfamiliar words. Lily wondered how she'd ever learned to read at all. Did she even attend school?

How could the world be full of so many lost little girls like Casey and Abby? Like McBride's Clare?

The vision seemed to last forever, through two more chapters of the book, through the lengthening of shadows in Casey's tiny bedroom. Just as Lily realized how long she'd been there, the door in her mind opened, beckoning her back to reality.

"You have to go." Casey put down her book and picked up her tattered stuffed frog. "It's okay. My daddy gave me Mr. Green to watch after me."

"I'll try to come back," Lily promised.

The sun-warmed vinyl seat of the rental car replaced the dank mists swirling around her. She opened her eyes to bright sunlight, her heart pounding against her rib cage. The dashboard clock read four-fifteen. Two hours had passed, just as they had in her vision.

Lily pressed her face into her hands, trying to reorient herself in a world that seemed surreal after the sweet cocoon of time she'd just spent with the sad-eyed little girl who called herself Casey. Who was this child? Why did she have such a strong connection with Lily, strong enough to draw her to a misty netherworld and keep her there for almost two hours when most of Lily's visions lasted no more than five or ten minutes?

She had to find out who Casey was, try to make sense of her part in what was happening to Abby Walters.

But first she had to deal with McBride.

McBride leaned over his kitchen table, his hand barely touching the smooth side of the unopened bottle of Jack Daniels. He couldn't remember buying it, couldn't even remember how or when he'd arrived at his house.

All he could remember was how hot and strong the whiskey had always felt as it washed down his throat and filled his stomach, numbing the pain, if only for a while.

He flipped another page of the photo album lying in front of him. He didn't remember bringing it out, either. He hadn't looked at it in a long time. He didn't know why he was doing so now. Every photograph was a fresh stab in the heart.

Clare at birth, tiny, red and wrinkled. Laura holding Clare, joy lighting her face from the inside. Clare's first birthday, when she'd put out the candle with her hand…

McBride shoved the album away and clutched the bottle of whiskey between his palms, rubbing the smooth glass surface to warm the golden liquid inside. Four years of sobriety were about to head out the window. He needed numbness so badly he thought he might die if he didn't take one drink.

He wanted it almost as much as he wanted Lily.

He'd thought that once he ended it, he could just walk away. But she was like a splinter, driving deeper the more he tried to extract her. He bled inside from wanting her.

Like the alcohol, she promised heat and release. Relief from pain, at least for a while. He could almost taste her on his tongue, feel her slick heat welcome him deep inside her.

He could pour the Jack Daniels down the sink and the craving would eventually leave him alone, at least for a while. But even though he'd chased Lily away, he couldn't escape her. And that scared the hell out of him.

The front doorbell rang. He ignored it and tore the paper seal around the neck of the bottle.

The bell rang again, long and persistent.

"Go away!" he yelled.

The person at the door started banging. Hard. Relentlessly.

Anger poured through McBride, the first thing he'd felt besides grief in hours. He liked the feeling. He lunged to his feet, slamming the bottle of whiskey down on the kitchen counter on his way to the living room. He threw the dead bolt latch and jerked open the door, ready for a fight.

The sight of Lily hit him like cold water in the face. He staggered back from the door.

She took a step toward him, her expression wary. "You don't get to end this by yourself."

He took another step back. "Go away."

"No." She crossed to him and took his hands. Hers were soft and warm, her touch sending sensations coursing through him like a powerful drug.

He stiffened, resisting. "No."

She lifted one hand to his face. Something inside him cracked and spilled out, spreading warmth through his chest. In the face of her tender persistence, his resolve began to crumble. When she slipped her arms around him, he leaned heavily against her and let her lead him to the sofa.

She stroked and soothed him, cradling his face between her palms. She drew his head down and kissed him, her lips warm and incredibly soft. The coldness inside him began to recede, coiling back into its hidden lair. She deepened their kiss, touching her tongue to his. He opened his mouth to her gentle invasion, gave in to the electric sensations sparking in his belly and loins.

Lily curled her fingers into the fabric of his shirt and murmured his name. He covered her mouth with his, swallowing the word. Desire scorched through him as he drew her to her feet, pulling her with him toward his bedroom.

They didn't make it out of the living room.

Chapter Thirteen

McBride pressed Lily against the living room wall and ran his hands down her thighs, drawing them apart to cradle the hardening ridge of his erection. Heat pooled in her center as he rolled his hips, baring his teeth in primitive satisfaction when she gasped at the electric sensation.

He rocked against her, the friction shooting sparks along her spine. Unbearable anticipation built inside her.

Tightening his grip on her with one hand, he tugged open the zipper of her pants, then pushed both jeans and panties over her hips to bare her flesh to him.

She needed more. Now.

He tangled his hand in the curls between her thighs, his fingers teasing the sensitive flesh until she shook with need. Kicking away the clothes tangled around her feet, she opened herself to his touch. He knew how and where to stroke her, when to tease and when to torture. When he slid two fingers inside her, she clutched his shoulders and growled his name.

He silenced her with another hard kiss, unzipping his own pants. Savage need coiled inside her as he grasped her hips and held her steady. His gaze locked with hers, his eyes black with passion. Her breath caught in her throat. Then he rose between her thighs and drove into her in one long, hard thrust. She dug her fingernails into his back, gasping at the sudden fullness.

He went still, searching her face. "Lily…"

She kissed away the uncertainty her soft cry had elicited. "Please," she whispered, sliding her hands over his shoulders and down his back. She pressed her palms against his buttocks and pulled him deeper into her. A low groan of pleasure rumbled up her throat.

He stroked her breasts lightly through her blouse, his thumb teasing her nipples to aching peaks. She arched against him, felt him stir deep inside her. Her belly quivered and softened as he began to move within her.

He unbuttoned her blouse, unsnapped her bra and pushed both garments aside, covering her bare breasts with his palms. As he stroked her, gentled her with his caresses, she relaxed, accepting more of him with each thrust.

A delicious tension began to build in her core. She found his rhythm and rocked with him, stoking the fire spreading through her belly.

He pulled her thighs up, lifting her feet off the floor. She held on to him tightly, wrapping her legs around his waist as he pinned her against the wall. He soon lost control, his thrusts hard and frantic, and she realized he was going to finish well ahead of her.

He gave one final upward lunge and his body went rigid as he found release. Her name trembled on his lips, soft and desperate as a prayer, and she didn't care that her own body still buzzed with tension, unfulfilled. For this moment, at least, she'd given him exactly what he needed.

It was what she'd come here to do.

MCBRIDE DIDN'T KNOW HOW much time passed before he was able to move again. Lily's fingers convulsed against his back, her hips still moving slightly against him. He stroked her hair and brushed his mouth against hers, tasting her tears. "It's okay," he whispered, wondering if it was. It had been a long time since he'd been with a woman, but not so long that he had forgotten what it felt like when she reached her climax.

Lily hadn't.

He lowered her feet to the floor and pulled away from her. She made a soft, rattling noise deep in her throat, and clung to him, not letting him release her.

He stroked her cheek, growing alarmed. "Lily?"

She lifted her hand to his face. "Shh."

Her gentle touch felt like an accusation. He could hardly bear to look at her. "I'm sorry. I just—I needed—"

She pressed her lips to his. "I know."

He should have gone slow, taken time to find out what pleased her. To make love to her with his hands and mouth, readying her for him, giving her pleasure before taking his own.

She took his hand and moved toward the hallway. When he resisted, she met his gaze, her eyes dark with need and a hint of laughter. "Don't dawdle. You have unfinished business."

His heart stopped, then restarted at a jackhammer pace. Grasping her hand, he led her to his bedroom.

FULL DARKNESS HAD FALLEN when Casey woke. She hadn't meant to fall asleep, but she'd kept reading after Lily left, and suddenly her eyes just wouldn't stay open.

She sat up and yawned, looking at the thin crack of light under her closed door. Was Mama awake?

She crept to Mama's bedroom. The door was open, and she slipped inside. Mama was on the bed, still clothed, her shoes on her feet. She lay atop the covers, but Casey could tell by the slow rise and fall of her chest that she was asleep.

Maybe that was good, Casey thought. Maybe when morning came, Mama would be like she used to be, before her spells.

Casey tiptoed back to her bedroom, changed into her pajamas and curled up on the bed, cuddling Mr. Green close. Still groggy, she closed her eyes and tried to go to sleep. But she had a hollow feeling in her chest, as if she was all alone in the world. The feeling made her sad and a little scared. She wished she could go find Lily. Lily would make her feel better.

Or maybe Abby, she thought with a sudden smile. Abby probably had that empty, all-alone feeling, too. She was a lot littler than Casey, and she was always real scared because of the mean men who took her away from her daddy and mommy. Abby would probably like Casey to come see her.

Casey didn't have words or thoughts to explain how she could visit Abby and Lily in her mind. She just could. She had thought they might be like her other friends, the ones she played with in her mind. There was Fern, who had a white poodle named Juliet. And Sam, who had a cat named Moonshine and a daddy who was a sea captain. She'd read about all her friends, knew what they looked like from the pictures in the books or from her own imagination.

But she'd never read about Abby or Lily. Lily had

appeared to her first, a brief flash in her mind as she lay in bed, somewhere between sleeping and waking. Curious, Casey had followed her through the gray mists to the room where Abby stayed. Casey had left when Lily did, but the next time she'd stayed and talked to Abby. Abby told her about her daddy and mommy and about how the bad men had grabbed her and hit her mommy and how her mommy had fallen down and gone to sleep.

Casey hadn't said the word *dead* to Abby, but that's what she thought. Abby's mommy was dead, like Casey's real mama.

But what about Daddy?

Casey could still hear his voice in her head sometimes. *Sweet baby marshmallow, close your bright eyes....*

Casey grabbed Mr. Green and squeezed his lumpy body to hers. She curled into a little knot, her forehead creasing with concentration. She tried to imagine the mists surrounding her, like on a foggy day, when she couldn't see her hand in front of her face. She drifted through the fog, looking for Abby.

She found Abby's room, smelled the musty, dirty scent. But Abby wasn't in there.

Fear coiled in Casey's chest. Was she with the bad men?

Then she saw the open window. The sunflower curtain rippled in the cool breeze flowing through it. Casey let herself float to the window to look out at the meadow of tall grass stretching to the edge of thick, dark woods. She spotted Abby, a speck of light in the darkness. She'd crawled out of the window! She'd gotten away from the bad men! Casey clapped her hands and laughed. Yea, Abby!

Suddenly, the door behind Casey banged open. She

whirled around and saw a man filling the doorway. He had sandy hair, a mean, scowly look on his face and a big gun in his hand. Beyond him, two men lay on the floor. Something red pooled around them, as if they'd spilled cherry Kool-Aid and taken a nap in the middle of the mess.

Only Casey knew it wasn't really cherry Kool-Aid. It was darker and thicker and it smelled funny, like the bright pennies she collected in a little pink piggy bank on her dresser. She didn't like the way it smelled. It made her tummy feel all squirmy and hot.

The big man in the doorway rushed toward her, sending panic shooting through her veins. She crouched in terror, trying to make herself as small as she could.

He walked right through her, and she remembered with a gush of relief that she wasn't really there in the little room with the messy bed and the open window.

He peered out the window. Could he see Abby?

Casey joined him at the window, keeping her distance even though she knew now that he couldn't see her. Outside, Abby had disappeared from view. Relief washed through Casey, making the room glitter like fairy dust and almost disappear.

She focused her mind on staying in the room, braced by her growing worry about Abby alone in the woods. Now Lily wouldn't know where to find her. And anything could happen to a little girl all alone. Didn't Mama always tell her that, back when Mama used to talk to her more?

She had to follow Abby so she wouldn't be alone. That was all there was to it. And later, maybe she could find Lily and tell her where Abby was now. Lily would know what to do. She'd know how to stop the bad man with the scowly face and the gun.

Lily would take care of them.

LILY NESTLED NEXT TO McBride under the warm quilt and listened to his heartbeat beneath her cheek. She could never turn back now. Making love to him had only sealed their fate. She just had to figure out how to make things work for them outside the bedroom.

"This isn't how I thought today would end," McBride murmured against her neck.

"You're not sorry, are you?"

He sat up, drawing her into his arms. "No. You?"

"No." She pressed her mouth against the faint cleft of his chin. "But since you brought up the subject of today…"

He drew away slightly. "Do we have to talk about it?"

She wasn't going to give in. McBride needed this. She scooted to the headboard and draped her arm around his broad shoulders. "Start with Laura. Where did you meet her?"

He turned to look at Lily, his features tinged with reluctance. But after a moment, he relaxed a little, leaned into her embrace.

"College," he answered. "She was great at math. I was good at history. We sort of bartered with each other. She helped me in math and I got her through Western Civ."

"What did she look like?"

He smiled, his eyes distant. "Cute. Not movie star pretty, but cute. She had the prettiest skin, very fair. I remember she always wore about a ton of sunscreen whenever she walked out the door. Clare had the same kind of skin."

Once McBride got started, the story poured out of him. He told Lily about the friendship that had turned into romance. The marriage right after graduation. Laura had taught junior high math and he'd gone straight to the police academy. After three years of marriage, they'd started trying to have a baby, but Laura couldn't carry to term.

"A fertility expert finally found a deformity in her uterus that other doctors missed. It was a fairly simple surgical procedure. Next thing we knew, we had Clare."

His mouth tightened when he said his daughter's name. Lily squeezed his shoulders, wishing she had her sister Iris's gift. Iris could have absorbed his pain and eased his suffering. Lily would've given anything to take away McBride's pain.

But all she could do was see things that other people couldn't, a gift McBride loathed. And after seeing him with Delaine this afternoon, hearing how the woman's broken promises had ripped his life apart, Lily understood why.

"How old was Clare when she disappeared?" she asked.

"Barely three."

Just a baby, Lily thought.

"She was there, playing in the yard one minute, and the next…" His voice grew faint, as if he couldn't believe it any more now than he could six years ago. "Gone. Just like that."

"Nobody saw anything?"

He shook his head. "It was a weekday. Most of the families on the street had older kids, all in school. Laura had been teaching Clare to ride her tricycle when the phone rang. Laura ran inside to get it. She wasn't gone more than a minute or two. We had a fenced-in yard." His voice broke. "She didn't think anything could happen."

Lily closed her eyes, heartsick. Maybe she'd been wrong to make him tell her these things.

He drew his legs up to his chin, curling in on himself. "It was Laura's idea to work with a psychic, but I didn't argue. I'd have done anything to find Clare."

"So you found Delaine."

"She found us. She came to the station and said she'd had a vision about Clare. She knew what Clare had been wearing and about a scrape on her chin where she'd fallen off her trike. She knew about her favorite toy. God, we wanted to believe her," he said bitterly.

"Of course. You wanted to find your daughter."

"We wanted somebody to tell us that she was all right, even after weeks passed without any leads." He rubbed his jaw with a shaky hand. "I'm a policeman, Lily. I knew the truth. It was staring me in the face, but I couldn't deal with it. Delaine convinced us that she'd seen Clare, that she was living with another family and all we had to do was find out who those people were. She kept having visions, getting closer and closer, and I believed every single word she said.

"I followed every clue, stayed up all night for days on end, going over every detail, considering all the possibilities. If she saw a rose in her vision, I'd make a list of all the florists and nurseries in the state. I'd even look for the name Rose in the phone book, just in case. I did legwork and more legwork, knocked on doors, made phone calls, hounded my fellow cops until they were ready to have me put away, and finally—finally!" His laugh was the most horrible sound Lily had ever heard. "Delaine had a breakthrough. She saw Clare in a green-and-white house over in Rockwell, just over the county line. She even gave us a name. The Graingers."

"So you found the Graingers?" Goose bumps scattered across Lily's bare shoulders.

"We converged on the place. Two cars from here, plus the county sheriff over in Rockwell. Lights flashing, sirens going. Scared the hell out the poor Graingers, who were having a birthday party for their little girl."

"Who wasn't Clare."

"Who wasn't Clare." His voice sounded dead. "Because Clare was dead. I think I realized it the instant I saw the little Grainger girl with her pigtails and pretty green party dress. Holly Grainger was alive. My baby was dead."

"I'm so sorry." Tears spilled down Lily's cheeks.

"After that, I told Delaine to stay away from us. I forbade her to go anywhere near Laura. I made sure she wasn't allowed at the station house." He sighed. "What she did to us was the cruelest thing she could've done. She should have just killed us instead."

Lily felt sick, understanding so much that had puzzled her since she'd first met him. She wondered how he could bear to be around her after his experience with Delaine. No wonder he wanted her to stay away from Andrew.

Yet she knew Abby Walters was alive. She *knew* it.

But had Delaine been equally sure about Clare?

"After the incident at the Graingers', Laura started seeing Clare everywhere. At the grocery store, the park, at church. She'd drive by schools and swear she saw her playing on the swings or climbing the monkey bars." His chest heaved, as if the mere effort to breathe was too much for him. "One day, she thought she saw Clare across Beaumont Parkway. She didn't even look before she ran into the street. There was a car—"

Lily couldn't bear to hear any more. She pressed her hand over McBride's mouth. "Please!"

He pulled her hand away as if compelled to finish. "I got to the emergency room just before she died. The last thing she told me was that she'd seen Clare. She wanted me to go get her." His face crumpled. "I couldn't do the last thing she wanted me to do. I couldn't go get our baby."

A hard, gasping sob exploded from him, wrenched from the dark place Lily had sensed in him almost from the first. She held him, aching for the child he had loved and she'd never gotten the chance to know, while he emptied himself of six years of darkness.

His shudders subsided gradually, and he drew away from her. She let go, giving him time to compose himself. He sat on the edge of the bed with his back to her, his hands moving his eyes to wipe away the evidence of his grief. "I'm sorry."

"Don't be."

He looked at her over his shoulder. "I know you believe you're really seeing Abby Walters when you go into your trance or whatever it is. I know that."

"But you don't believe it."

"I don't have it in me anymore." He ran his hand over his jaw. "I'm sorry."

"It's okay."

He turned away from her. "You'll start to resent me."

Was he right? At this moment, in his bed, with his body warm and solid beside her, she couldn't imagine it.

But what would happen the next time she had a vision of Abby?

Lily had run from her gift her whole life, had hated it, feared it. Now she'd finally begun to trust herself, to believe she had been given this special ability for a purpose. She could use it to help people, find scared little girls like Abby.

She couldn't turn back now. Even when she had run from it, the gift had been a fundamental element of who she was.

It defined her.

McBride turned and touched her face. "Let's not think about any of this tonight, okay? We'll think about it later." He lay down and pulled her into his arms, his breath warm against her cheek. She heard his breathing deepen as he drifted off to sleep, his body relaxed and content behind hers.

But she lay awake, wondering if their newfound intimacy could outlast her next vision.

Chapter Fourteen

Casey couldn't feel the cold as she followed Abby into the woods, but she knew the smaller girl had to be freezing. She wore no coat and only a pair of thin, dirty socks on her feet. Older and wiser, Casey felt the weight of responsibility for her friend. She had to help Abby find a warm, safe place to stay until Casey could find a way to reach Lily.

"Abby!" she cried. Abby kept running.

She must be scared of the scowly man with the gun, Casey thought, straining to catch up. She glanced over her shoulder to see if the man was following. She couldn't spot him, but she heard crashing noises in the woods behind her. Fear rose in her chest, hot and sharp. It tasted like pennies, reminding her of the men she'd left behind in the trailer.

Ahead, Abby dashed through the woods, tripping on tree roots and getting tangled in the low bushes blanketing the forest floor. She somehow stayed just out of reach, and Casey couldn't figure out why. After all, Casey was floating along like a butterfly, easily staying clear of the stumps and vines that made Abby fall down over and over.

"Abby, you've gotta hide! I can help!" Casey screamed into the darkness. *Oh, God, please help her hear me,* she prayed fervently. *Make her hear me.*

Abby tripped over another root and sprawled forward, hitting the ground with a thud. She made soft, gasping noises that scared Casey into a final spurt of effort.

"Abby, are you okay? Abby, can you hear me?" Casey finally touched her friend.

The little girl managed to draw a few short, struggling breaths. The wheezy sounds subsided and her eyes widened. "Casey?"

Casey felt like cheering. "Shh! Yeah, it's me! You got away from them but somebody's coming after you!"

Abby started crying. "I heard a bang-bang noise, Casey. I think it was a gun!"

Casey thought of the weapon she'd seen in the scowly man's hand. It had looked gigantic, like a cannon.

"They're gonna find me," Abby mewled. "They're gonna come after me and shoot me!" She choked on her sobs. "Tell me what to do, Casey! I'm scared."

"You've gotta be quiet, like Lily tells you, 'member?"

Abby's sniffles sounded like thunder in Casey's ears. "I want Lily!" the little girl wailed. Even though the words came from Abby's mind, not her mouth, Casey held her breath, afraid the scowly man had heard.

"It's okay," she promised, her own thoughts a whisper. "Lily will be here, you wait and see."

BY MIDNIGHT LILY WAS still awake, too tense to close her eyes. Her stomach growled, reminding her she'd skipped dinner.

Without waking McBride, she extracted herself from

his grasp and slid out of bed. Cool air washed over her body, raising chill bumps, so she slipped on his discarded shirt and picked up the extra blanket that had fallen on the floor during their lovemaking, wrapping it around herself before heading to the kitchen to find something to eat.

The pantry wasn't well stocked. After moving a few boxes and cans, she found a pack of crackers that didn't look too old. She grabbed a glass from the draining rack by the sink, filled it with water and carried her snack to the table.

Halfway there, she felt the shivers hit. She made it to the table, falling into one of the chairs just before the door in her mind crashed open and she was sucked into the mists.

Casey appeared in the fog in front of her. "Oh, Lily!" She flung herself into her arms.

"What is it?" Lily squeezed her close.

"There was a gunshot, and a bad scowly man had a gun, and I think he killed the bad men who took Abby, and she got away but she's all alone in the woods and it's cold and she's scared, and he's looking for her, and I don't know what to do!" Casey squirmed out of Lily's embrace and tugged her hand urgently. "You've got to help us!"

Lily didn't wait for Casey's words to sink in, tightening her grip on the child's hand, she followed her through the mist.

McBride lay between dozing and waking, waiting for Lily to return to bed. Though her scent lingered in the sheets and on his skin, he missed the feel of her next to him.

He pressed his face against her pillow and breathed

deeply, remembering the way her soft, spicy-sweet scent had washed over him during their lovemaking. She had been both generous and demanding, trusting him enough to let him know when he was pleasing her and when she needed more. She'd given back to him in return, eager and willing to please him, as well.

And afterward, she'd given him what he'd needed most, letting him share the darkness he'd kept inside for so long.

He had been terrified of letting go of his grief, as if in doing so he would lose what small connection he had left with Laura and Clare. But he hadn't lost them, after all. For the first time since Clare's disappearance, he found he could think of his daughter and smile, too.

Clare had been a happy child, full of joy and laughter. She could flash her dimples at him and make his heart melt. He had almost forgotten that over the past six years.

How could he have let his rage and grief steal Clare's smiles from him?

Thanks to Lily, he had those memories back again.

Tired of waiting for her to return to bed, he slipped on a pair of pants and followed the light to the kitchen, where he found Lily sitting at the table, her back to him. He padded across the cold linoleum and lifted her hair, pressing his mouth against the side of her throat. "Hungry?" he asked, noting the crackers sitting in front of her.

She didn't answer.

Then he saw the glass lying on its side, water dribbling off the table and puddling on the floor at her feet. The skin on the back of his neck tingled. "Lily?"

He crouched next to her. Her forehead was creased, her eyes open but unseeing. A whisper passed between her soft pink lips, but he could make out no words.

She was having another vision.

Ignoring the spilled water, he sat across from her, his heart in his throat. He hadn't expected to have to deal with this part of her so soon. After all they'd just been through, he still couldn't—wouldn't—believe she had some sort of supernatural ability to "see" people and places beyond her own reality. Yet neither could he believe she was a liar, a charlatan putting on an act for his benefit.

So the only other option was what? Madness?

Her sightless eyes stared toward the kitchen window, but he knew she wasn't seeing her reflection in the darkened panes.

With growing unease, he waited.

"THERE SHE IS!" Casey pointed and tugged Lily's hand.

The mists in Lily's mind parted to reveal Abby, crying quietly in the middle of a dense, dark wood. The trees loomed over her like spindly monsters, dwarfing her tiny body. Lily intensified her concentration and touched the frightened child's tearstained face. She felt the dampness beneath her fingertips.

"Lily, you came!" Abby's face lit up with a smile. A now-familiar ripple of wonder shot through Lily. She knew that in reality she was sitting in a chair in McBride's kitchen, but she could feel Abby's soft skin as surely as if she were truly there in the dark, cold woods.

She soothed Abby as she concentrated on seeing more of the child's surroundings. The forest stretched into blackness, but she heard sounds in the distance, something—someone—crashing through the underbrush. Lily clenched her jaw and focused her mind on seeing beyond the void, but she could only hear the noises. "Abby, you need to hide."

"There's a big bush over there." Casey pointed.

Lily led Abby to the bush and crouched beside her. "Abby, I need you to be quiet as a mouse. Can you do that?"

The little girl nodded.

Casey hunkered down beside them, her wide hazel eyes fixed on Lily's face, as if waiting for the next instruction. The full weight of responsibility crashed down on Lily's shoulders.

The noise behind them grew louder, and Lily finally caught sight of the source. Though the darkness rendered him little more than a hulking shadow, she could tell by his build and his powerful movements that he was a man.

She peered through the gloom, wishing her gift of clairvoyance came with a built-in spotlight. She couldn't get a good look at him in the dark.

Until he came close enough to touch.

A thin beam of moonlight pierced the canopy of trees overhead, revealing his sandy hair and stocky build. Around forty, he wore dark clothes and carried a large gun.

Lily tightened her grip on Abby. The child went still.

The man crept closer. Lily held her breath, terrified he'd find Abby's hiding place.

After an excruciating length of time, he passed the bush where Abby was hidden. The little girl started to get up, but Lily held her in place, allowing herself to breathe again. She waited, caressing Abby's small arm, until the man was well away. Then she whispered, "Do you think you're ready to keep walking, Abby?"

"Sure she is." Casey took one of Abby's hands. "We can make it together, can't we?"

Abby blinked away her tears and nodded.

Lily helped Abby up. "Honey, you need to think hard, okay? Think hard about Casey and me holding your hands. Do you feel it?"

Abby nodded.

"Okay. Do you remember which direction you came from, sweetie?" The last thing Lily wanted was to lead the little girl back to her abductors.

Abby looked around. She lifted one plump arm and pointed. "Over there."

"She's right, that's the way we came," Casey agreed.

Lily tightened her fingers around Abby's hand. "Let's go."

By focusing sharply, she could see about fifty yards ahead of her at any one time, but thought it would be enough. She just had to keep Abby putting one foot in front of the other until they came to some sign of civilization.

After a long walk, Abby said, "I see a light."

Lily peered into the gloom, seeing nothing. "Which way?"

The little girl gestured to her left. She tugged Lily's hand, urging her to quicken her pace.

On the other side of Abby, Casey's image was wavery, not quite there. All of Lily's concentration was on Abby, which meant that Casey was sustaining her presence almost completely on her own. Lily wondered if the little girl was clairvoyant.

How was she ever going to explain this to McBride?

Suddenly, ahead, she saw it. A yellow light. It flickered as they approached, sometimes shielded by tree limbs but growing ever closer. Soon, Lily could make out the edge of a clearing, then the dark outline of some sort of building.

"It's a house!" Abby started running toward the light.

It was, indeed, a house. Made of natural pine clapboard, it nestled in a clearing in the woods, with a wide porch that spanned the entire front.

Abby almost tripped but caught herself, her little legs churning as she hurried forward.

Excitement surged through Lily as she realized that Abby was really going to be safe. She would knock on the door of that house and nice people would come to the door and help her.

Wouldn't they?

Or was Abby about to walk into the lair of an even more heinous monster?

Lily pushed her doubts to the back of her mind. Abby couldn't last out in the cold much longer. She had to take a chance on the people in this cabin. "Abby, knock on the door. Tell whoever answers that your name is Abby Walters and that you were kidnapped. Tell them to call the police, and tell them about yourself, okay? Can you remember all that?"

Abby nodded, her eyes bright with tears of nervous excitement. "Are you coming with me?"

"I can't, honey. But I'll come find you soon, I promise." She let go of Abby's hand.

As soon as the contact was broken, she felt the mists swirling around her, blurring the edges of her vision. Frantically she clung to the vision, watching Abby climb the three steps to the porch. Lily looked for some kind of distinguishing mark on the house so she could tell the police where to search for her.

As the mists encroached on the clearing around her, she caught sight of a painted wooden plaque hanging on the wall next to the front door of the house—geese flying in tandem, a wide blue banner stretched between their beaks. In neat script on the banner was written The Marlins.

Then the mist swallowed her. She emerged from the grayness a few seconds later.

But she wasn't in McBride's kitchen.

She was in Casey's bedroom.

"You're going to leave me now, aren't you?" Casey stood before her, arms tight around her tattered green frog.

"I promise I'll try to come back. Maybe you can help me do that."

Casey smiled. "I don't feel alone when you're here."

Lily tried to hug the little girl, but the tug of reality at her back was too strong. Arms still outstretched to Casey, she was sucked back through the door in her mind.

Casey gazed out at her from the doorway, tears trickling down her cheeks. Then the door slammed shut and Lily was back in the kitchen. Looking at McBride.

She gave a little start.

His touch on her arm was tentative. "Are you okay?"

She clutched his wrist. "McBride, Abby got away from her kidnappers!"

His forehead creased with a frown. "Lily—"

"Please, you have to listen to me just this one time! Abby escaped through the window of the trailer home where they were keeping her. There was a man—I think maybe he killed Abby's kidnappers, and now he's looking for her in the woods. He has a gun. I helped Abby hide until he went past us, then we walked in the other direction and found a house in the woods. The last I saw of Abby, she was knocking on the door."

Brow furrowed, McBride stood up and took a step away from her.

She followed, closing the gap he'd opened. "You've got to call the FBI or somebody! What if the people at that house aren't nice?"

"You sound…crazy."

"Damn it, McBride, if you don't call someone, I'm going to do it. She's at a house in the woods. I couldn't get a good bearing as to where it might be, but I think it's here in this county. The terrain looks kind of familiar. The house is one-story, pine clapboard, with a big veranda-style porch. And there's a plaque on the wall by the front door, two flying geese carrying a banner with The Marlins printed on it."

He grabbed her hand. "Lily, listen to me—"

Before he could say another word, the phone rang.

A bubble of hope rose in Lily's throat. Had the people in the house already called the police?

McBride didn't move for a moment. She could tell by his expression that the timing of the call spooked him a little. He looked from her to the ringing phone.

"Get it." Her stomach tightened with anticipation.

He crossed to the phone. "McBride."

Seconds later, myriad emotions darted over his face—disbelief, anger, confusion, consternation, realization, bewilderment and, finally, a mixture of fear and hope. "Okay, I'm on my way." He hung up the phone.

"It's Abby, isn't it?"

He walked slowly toward her, looking stunned. "A man named Jerry Marlin called the county sheriff. A little girl knocked on his door in the middle of the night, said she was Abby Walters and they were supposed to call the police."

It took a second for McBride's words to sink in. Then

shivers rolled over Lily. She groped behind her for the chair and sat. "She's okay?"

"Best they can tell." As McBride closed the distance between them, he opened his mouth, then closed it again, as if he didn't know what to say.

Neither did she.

He stopped a foot in front of her. "Agent Brody is headed out there already. I've got to go."

She pushed away from the table. "I'm going with you."

MCBRIDE CONCENTRATED on the dark, winding road. Jerry Marlin's address was a rural route box, but the sheriff had given him good directions. They were less than a mile away now.

Lily had been silent during the drive. Just as well. McBride didn't know what to say to her. The world was upside down, nothing making much sense. He was a man who dealt in facts. The facts of the Abby Walters case were that the little girl apparently was alive, after all. She'd apparently escaped her captors, made her way through the woods and knocked on the door of Jerry Marlin's cabin.

And Lily Browning had told him every single fact well before the phone rang.

He was afraid to believe that he was about to see Abby Walters alive and well. He'd been sure they'd find her in a ditch or a Dumpster somewhere around the county. He'd been rehearsing the words he would say to Andrew Walters.

He was afraid to believe until he saw Abby for himself.

He pulled off the highway onto a gravel road that led deep into the woods. The gravel soon gave way to dirt. "Almost there," he murmured, the first words he'd said in ten minutes.

Next to him, Lily was tense and pale. She turned to look at him, her eyes glittering in the dashboard lights.

"How you doing?" he asked. "Warm enough?"

She nodded. "Did anybody call Andrew Walters?"

He shook his head. "We want to wait, make sure this isn't a hoax or a false alarm." The Chevy's headlights suddenly picked up the reflector paint on a county sheriff's car, then the pine cabin looming just beyond. McBride parked behind the sheriff's cruiser and turned to Lily. "Ready?"

She unbuckled her seat belt and nodded.

They converged in front of the car, Lily sliding her hand into his. He tightened his fingers around hers and walked with her up the shallow porch steps. Immediately he saw the wooden plaque beside the front door. Even in the waning moonlight, he could make out the pair of geese and the printed banner. "The Marlins," he murmured.

Lily's hand trembled in his. He looked down at her and saw her staring at the plaque. "It's really here," she breathed.

He squeezed her hand and knocked on the door. It opened and a lanky black sheriff's deputy greeted him. "You McBride?"

"Yes." He indicated the shield on his belt, then released Lily's hand. "This is Lily Browning. She's been helping us on the case. Where's the child?"

The deputy waved toward a doorway to the left. McBride went through the wide archway, Lily right behind him.

Three people sat at the kitchen table. A burly man with steel-gray hair was in one chair, a short, plump woman with pink curlers in her bleached hair across from him.

And in the middle, her grubby little hands wrapped around a stoneware mug, sat Abby Walters.

McBride's stomach tightened into a hard, hot ball. He took a couple of tentative steps toward the child, then closed the rest of the distance in a dash, reaching out to touch the little girl's face. "Abby?"

She blinked rapidly, startled by his sudden approach.

Her skin was warm and unbelievably soft. He drew a swift breath. "Tell me your name, honey."

She wiped her cheek with one grimy hand. "I'm Abby Walters, I live at 524 Winslow Road and I want to go home."

"Your daddy will be here soon. But I need you to tell me everything you remember about tonight."

Abby's face crumpled. "I heard a bang. It sounded like a big firecracker going off. I pushed and pushed at the window and it opened, so I climbed out and ran."

McBride glanced over his shoulder at Lily. She stood in the kitchen doorway, her arms wrapped tightly around her stomach, tears in her eyes as she stared at Abby.

She had been right about everything. Skeet, Gordy, Abby. This house and the geese on the plaque on the porch…

He looked back at Abby, who was saying, "It was real high and I was scared I'd fall and break my neck like Mama always says, but I was more scared Skeet'd come get me and hit me like he hit my mama, and so I opened the window and I jumped."

Her gaze shifted, looking beyond him.

He heard Lily's voice, soft and trembling. "Abby. It's Lily."

Abby's face lit up. She leaped from the table, pushing past McBride.

He turned in time to see the little girl fling herself into Lily's arms. Lily crushed the child to her, tears streaming down her cheeks.

"You came, Lily, you came!" Abby cried.

Chapter Fifteen

Lily tightened her arms around Abby. She was really here, really okay. Not just a tiny freckled face in the mists of her mind, but solid little arms and legs wrapped around her.

Abby patted Lily's cheeks with her hands. "You're so pretty! I never could see you."

Lily stroked Abby's red curls. "I'm so proud of you. You were such a brave girl to get away."

"Mama will be real proud of me, won't she?"

Lily's heart broke. She glanced past Abby to McBride, who leaned heavily against the table, watching them. He looked as if a truck had hit him.

All his firmly held, highly logical beliefs had just been blown apart. Abby was alive and well, and Lily had been dead on target. His whole sense of reality was probably off-kilter right now.

Agents Brody and Logan entered the kitchen behind her. Brody glared at Lily. "What's she doing here?"

"We've got a lot of ground to cover." McBride pushed himself away from the table edge. "Has anyone called Walters?"

Brody ignored Lily and smiled at Abby, his stony face softening. "You must be Abby."

The little girl tightened her grip on Lily.

"It's okay." Lily stroked the child's tousled curls. "Mr. Brody just needs to ask you some questions."

"About Gordy and Skeet?" Abby asked solemnly.

Lily threaded her fingers through Abby's hair. "Yes, honey. Let's go sit at the table and talk to Mr. Brody and Mr. Logan." She carried Abby to the table and set her in the chair.

"Ms. Browning?" Logan took Lily's arm as she started to sit by Abby. "I have some questions, if you don't mind."

"She was with me all night," McBride interjected.

Brody and Logan both turned to look at him, then back at Lily. A blush rolled up her neck and into her cheeks.

"Humor me," Brody said finally.

McBride started to protest, but Lily put her hand on his arm. "It's okay."

She followed Agent Logan to the parlor. He waved at the overstuffed settee by the window and took the paisley armchair across from her. His broad shoulders knocked awry the lace doily draped over the chair back. "Ms. Browning, tell me what happened after you left your house this evening."

"At least part of what I did is none of your business."

She was pleased to see that some men were still capable of blushing. "So tell me the part that is my business," he said.

Stifling a smile, Lily complied.

"YOU ACTUALLY HEARD LILY in your room, Abby?" Brody's voice was gentle, but McBride detected the steely edge.

"She wasn't really *in* the room." Abby's mouth tightened with impatience. "She was in my *mind,* helping me hear her."

"Did Lily tell you she was just in your mind?"

"Yeah, 'cause at first I thought she was a ghost voice and I was scared. But then she said she was in my mind, and I wasn't so scared. She hugged me and made me feel better."

"Hugged you? You felt her touch you?"

Abby frowned. "Well, sorta. It was like butterflies, you know? Like a hundred hundred butterflies flapping their wings against me. But it made me feel like I wasn't alone."

"And she helped you find this house?" Brody asked.

"She and Casey did. Lily said go knock on the door and tell them I was Abby Walters and to call the police." Abby nodded solemnly. "And I did."

McBride drew a shaky breath. Had Lily been with Abby in her mind, helping her find safety? What other explanation was there? Lily hadn't been out of his sight for fifteen minutes. Short of thumbing a ride on a passing helicopter, she couldn't have gotten to these woods and back in that short a time.

"Who's Casey?" Brody asked.

"She's this kid who came to visit me. I couldn't see her, either." Abby spoke as if she were saying nothing unusual.

Goose bumps rose on McBride's arms.

Brody glanced up at him, one brow cocked so high it almost reached his hairline. He looked back at the little girl. "Abby, are you sure Lily was never really in your room?"

"Yes, I'm sure. Neither was Casey. I told you." Abby's bottom lip puffed out and tears welled in her red-rimmed eyes. "I don't want to talk anymore. I wanna go home." Tears trickled from her eyes. "I want to see my mommy."

"Come on, Brody, she's had enough for tonight." McBride put his hand on the fed's arm. Brody motioned for McBride to follow him while Mrs. Marlin entered the room and comforted Abby.

"Who do you think this Casey is?" McBride asked as they stepped into the dark hallway.

Brody ignored the question. "Is Mr. Walters on his way?"

McBride nodded. "I sent a uniform to drive him here. He sounded too shaky to get here under his own steam."

"Good." Brody nodded and walked toward the open parlor door, a rectangle of light in the narrow, gloomy hall. McBride followed him. Inside, Lily and Agent Logan sat across from each other, both silent and tense.

"Mike, I'd like to see you out here for a minute," Brody said.

As Agent Logan came out of the parlor, McBride went inside and crouched next to Lily. "Everything okay?"

She nodded. "How's Abby holding up?"

"She's doing great. She thinks you're the best, you know." He didn't ask about Casey. Not in front of the agents. He'd save that for later.

Lily smiled. "I'm just glad she's okay."

"McBride, can I see you a moment?" Brody asked. He and Logan stepped away from the doorway, forcing McBride to follow them. Brody's grim expression made McBride's gut coil into an aching knot. The FBI agent lowered his voice. "We just got a call from your men. They found the trailer where Abby was being kept. We also found Debra Walters's missing Lexus."

McBride could tell there was more. "And the kidnappers?"

"Dead from gunshot wounds."

McBride remembered Lily's earlier words. A man with a gun.

Lily had seen a killer.

HE'D NEVER KILLED BEFORE.

It wasn't like he'd thought it would be, the kick of the gun in his hand or the sound ringing in his deafened ears. And the blood. God, the blood.

He'd had to do it. Make a mess to clean up the mess.

Blood spatter dotted his clothing, a fine red spray on the dark wool. But he'd been prepared for that possibility. He stripped off his latex gloves and wadded them up with his sweater, pants and shoes, shivering as the cool October breeze whipped across his bare skin. Tucking the bloodstained clothes into a small garbage bag, he tossed them into the Dumpster in the alley.

Donning the spare clothes he'd brought with him, he closed the top of the trash bin and returned to his car, his heart pounding with growing apprehension.

Had Abby seen him? He didn't think so. Even if she had, she was just a little girl, easily confused. And his alibi, should he need one, was rock solid.

Maybe it was finally over.

WALTERS ARRIVED at the Marlins' house around the time that Brody and Logan were briefing McBride on the two murders, so McBride missed the reunion between father and daughter. Walters was bundling the sleepy little girl into his arms when McBride and Lily reentered the kitchen.

Walters looked at Lily, his eyes bright with tears. "I don't know how…"

She shook her head and squeezed his hand. "Not necessary."

"Mr. Walters, I'd like to put you both in protective custody until things get settled."

Walters's blue eyes narrowed. "Settled how?"

McBride glanced at Abby, who'd already fallen asleep on her father's shoulder. Quietly, he told him about the murders.

Walters looked shocked. "My God. Why?"

That was the big question. Who would want to kill the kidnappers and why? "We're looking into that right now."

"And you think Abby's in danger?"

"She didn't see whoever shot the men, and as far as we know, he didn't see her. But we shouldn't take any chances." It was possible the sandy-haired man didn't consider Abby enough of a threat to go after her, but McBride wasn't ready to risk her life on that assumption. "We can provide twenty-four hour guard at your hotel room."

Walters shook his head. "I don't want her to stay in another strange place. Debra's sister agreed to take Abby until I can settle everything here. I'll send half my security detail with them. It'll free you up to find out who did this and why."

McBride would have preferred to keep Abby where he could make sure she was safe, but he understood Walters's need to get the girl into a familiar place with someone she knew and loved. "We may need to talk to her again."

Walters didn't look happy, but he nodded. "Understood."

McBride motioned Theo Baker over and briefed him on the plan, making it clear that he was to treat the trip back to the hotel as a protective detail.

McBride and Lily walked Walters and Abby out to Theo's car. The sergeant headed back around to the driver's seat. "You coming in to the office now?" he asked.

"I'm going to see Ms. Browning home." McBride didn't like the idea of leaving her alone, now that she was a murder witness.

Theo grinned. McBride's stern look only made his grin widen. "Just leave your cell phone on, Romeo."

When they'd left, McBride slid his arm around Lily's waist, leaning his head against hers. He was overjoyed to see Walters and his daughter reunited, but couldn't suppress a tinge of jealousy and resentment. Why hadn't he had a happy ending, too? He took a deep breath, careful to hide his feelings. "Hell of a night."

Lily slipped her arm around him. "A lot's happened that you need time to assimilate."

He looked at her. *Assimilate? Nice tidy word to describe having your entire mind turned inside out.* "You think?"

"Are you mad at me?" she asked.

He rubbed his face, ashamed of his snappishness. He was the one who'd been wrong, after all. He'd been wrong from the beginning, accusing her of being a liar and a fraud, then later thinking she was delusional.

Well, no avoiding it now. Lily was the genuine article, a visionary, a psychic, a clairvoyant—all those words he'd struck from his vocabulary years ago.

He just wished he felt better about it. Life had been simpler when he could bury himself in skepticism.

"I'm not mad." He touched her cheek. "I just need time."

"To assimilate." Her voice held a hint of amusement.

"Yeah."

Once they were back on the road, he asked the question that had nagged him since he'd listened to Abby Walters's story. "Lily, who's Casey?"

Her eyes glittered in the blue glow of the dashboard lights. "Abby mentioned her?"

The hair on his neck crawled. "She said Casey's a kid who visited her sometimes, but she never actually saw her."

"Casey is a little girl, about nine or ten. She lives with her mother, who's…odd." A thread of sadness ran through Lily's low voice. "I think maybe she's adopted, because her mother calls her by a different name."

A finger of unease ran down McBride's spine. "What name?"

"Gina."

An old, familiar ache of disappointment settled in his chest. "Where does she live?"

"I'm not sure. It could be anywhere."

"How'd she get to Abby's room?" He dreaded the answer.

"I think she's clairvoyant, too."

Great. "How many times have you seen her?"

Lily's eyes dropped. "A few."

"And you didn't tell me about her?"

She slanted her gaze at him in silent accusation.

Of course she hadn't. He'd have seen her story as proof she was a liar or a lunatic. "Why was Casey visiting Abby?"

Lily's voice darkened. "Maybe she's just a lonely little girl with a special gift, and she found Abby like you might find a particular radio station by flipping channels."

He fell silent and cranked the car, too wrung out to process one more strange, impossible fact tonight. Instead, he fell back on what he knew best. "You saw the man who killed Abby's kidnapper."

"I know. But he doesn't know that."

"If he reads the papers, he knows you're a psychic who was looking for Abby. That might be enough to put you in danger."

Her brow furrowed. "Then so is Casey. She saw him."

"But he couldn't see her, right? You said she wasn't really there."

His words elicited a faint smile. "I don't suppose anybody on your task force is eager to talk about her, either."

"No," he conceded. "But maybe you should talk to a sketch artist. Do you think you could describe the man you saw?"

She nodded. "But it won't be admissible in court. I can't exactly testify that I saw him in my mind."

Once again discomfort shuddered through him. He tamped it down. "I'd still like to see what you saw."

"So you believe me?"

The wary eagerness in her voice made his chest hurt. "Let's just say I'll consider the possibility," he answered. "I'll give Jim a call tomorrow morning and set something up."

"Not tonight?"

"It's almost 2:00 a.m. I think it can wait till morning."

"What *about* tonight?" Lily asked.

"You're coming home with me."

"Under protective custody? Or do you have something else in mind?" A smile curved her lips.

He shot her a heated gaze. "Oh, I have lots in mind."

BY THE TIME LILY ROLLED away from McBride, the glow of dawn was washing his bedroom, painting the walls and ceiling pink. Lily stared at the light patterns on the ceiling, trying to catch her breath.

McBride pushed her hair away from her face with a trembling hand. "See what you do to me?"

She smiled. "I love what I do to you. And I really, really love what you do to me."

He laughed. "Wanton hussy."

"I feel like a wanton hussy." She lifted herself onto one elbow. "I don't even know your first name."

He made a face. "I never use it. McBride's fine, really."

"Oh, come on. What is it?" She ran her finger down the dark line of hair that bisected his stomach.

He caught her hand and shook his head. "That dog won't hunt, sugar. Nobody calls me by my first name. Ever."

"I'll bet I can guess." She leaned on his chest and rubbed her chin against his sternum. "Is it James?"

"Nope."

"Jeremy, Joseph, Jud, Jed, Jeremiah, Jacob, Jesse?"

"Not even close." His smile broadened.

She frowned, frustrated. "Why don't you just tell me? For heaven's sake, you'd think it was Jubal or something!"

His grin collapsed like a pricked balloon.

Her eyes widened. "It's Jubal?"

He made a face. "Jubal is an honored McBride family name."

"Jubal." Grinning, she tried it out.

"Lily, nobody calls me Jubal."

"I'm starting to like it. Jubal." She pressed her mouth against his collarbone. "It could be my secret name for you."

His forehead creased. "Define 'secret name.'"

She nibbled the thick muscles of his neck. "Jubal," she whispered, flicking her tongue against his flesh. She dropped nipping little kisses along his neck and jaw, punctuating her soft murmurs. "Jubal, Jubal, Jubal—"

"Okay, I surrender." Laughing, he gently nudged her away from him. "You can call me Jubal. But only when we're alone." He held up a stern finger. "And only you. Nobody else knows."

"Not even my sister Rose?"

He looked horrified. "Especially not her!"

"Okay, it's our little secret." She bent to kiss him again, groaning when the phone on McBride's bedside table rang. "Damn it, who calls so early in the morning?"

"Goes with cop territory." He answered. "McBride."

Lily propped herself on her elbow again, watching the furrows in his brow deepen as he listened to whoever was on the line. "Okay, thanks. Stay in touch."

"What's up?" she asked when he hung up the phone.

McBride sat up and swung his legs over the side of the bed. "Let's find something to eat. Then I'll tell you all about it."

MAMA WAS ACTING FUNNY again, so Casey retreated to her bedroom, curling up with Mr. Green and escaping into *Boots and Belinda,* one of her favorite books. She'd read it so often now it was nearly falling apart, but if she turned the pages very carefully, she could still read it. She liked to pretend she was Belinda, who had a smart and brave cat named Boots.

One time Mama had brought home a kitten for Casey. They'd named him Patches because he had black and white spots all over. Mama had taught Casey how to hold him—not too tight, not too loose, but just right. That was back when Mama was a lot better.

But not long after that Mama started having more spells. Sometimes she'd forget to feed Patches or let him inside when it was cold. Patches finally left for good and Mama had never gotten Casey another cat.

But I'd never forget to feed a cat, Casey thought, draping the open book across her chest. *I'd feed her and change her water and brush her hair like Belinda brushes Boots.*

She smiled at the ceiling. She'd name her Lily, she thought. And maybe the real Lily would come visit. Then Casey could show her the kitty and say, "See, I named her after you! So you'll have to come visit all the time and play with her."

Casey rolled onto her side, suddenly sad. She had that all alone feeling again, now that Abby was back with her daddy and Casey couldn't find her anymore.

"Gina?" Mama's voice sliced through Casey's melancholy. She stood in the doorway, her blue eyes wide and strange. "I don't want you talking so loud anymore, young lady!"

Casey frowned. Talking loud? "I wasn't talking, Mama."

"Don't yell at me, young lady!" Mama lurched toward her. "If you can't behave, you'll just have to stay in here."

Casey clutched Mr. Green more tightly to her. "But Mama—"

Mama grabbed the doorknob and stepped back into the hall, pulling the heavy door shut behind her.

"I can't take any more of your screaming!" The door muffled Mama's voice. Casey heard a scraping noise, metal on metal. "I can't take it anymore!" Mama's voice rose with hysteria. Casey heard great, wracking sobs through the door.

She ran to the door and pressed her ear against it. She heard Mama's shuffling, unsteady footsteps retreat down the hall, accompanied by loud hiccups.

Quietly, carefully, Casey tried to turn the doorknob. It rattled uselessly in her hand. Locked. She tapped cautiously on the door. "Mama, can you hear me?"

Nothing but silence.

She rapped more loudly. "Mama, I'm scared. Please let me out." She pressed her ear to the door and waited for her reply. Still there was nothing.

She hugged Mr. Green closer and looked around the room, wondering what to do. There was no other door, no way out. She couldn't get out the window because it was painted tightly shut.

A shiver wracked her body. Daddy would know how to get her out. He'd say, "Sit tight, Casey, and I'll have you out in a jiffy." Yes sir, that's what he'd say if he was here.

But he wasn't here. Nobody was here but her and Mama.

"Mama, please come open the door. I'm hungry and I'm scared and I've got to pee."

Still nothing. No answer, no noise.

Little Abby found a way out, Casey reminded herself. She'd just climbed out her window and run for help, big as you please.

But she had had Casey's help. And Lily's.

Lily would know what to do, if only Casey could figure out a way to reach her. Clutching the stuffed frog against her chest, she squeezed her eyes shut and concentrated hard.

Lily!

"THEY IDENTIFIED THE bodies in the trailer as Rick 'Skeet' Scotero and Gordon 'Gordy' Stevens. Two-bit career criminals with records going back twenty years." McBride hunted through the cabinets for something to eat.

"Any idea why they took her?" Lily asked.

"Brody thinks someone hired the men to threaten Debra Walters and her daughter. They're rounding up Senator Blackledge and his campaign staff as we speak." He turned to look at her. "I called the sketch artist. He'll meet us at your house at ten this morning. But don't tell anyone else you saw the man in the woods. We don't know who he's connected to. No point putting yourself in more danger. Agreed?"

"That makes sense." Lily started to push aside the blue binder on the table when she realized it was a photo album. Curiosity battled dread. But she was incapable of leaving it closed. She shot a glance at McBride. He was crouched by the cabinets next to the sink, sorting through some cans.

Hands trembling, she opened the album to the first photo.

It was an eight-by-ten family portrait. McBride, Laura and a small baby. *Clare,* Lily thought, her tears blurring the chubby little face. She wiped them away.

All three were smiling, McBride's face carefree and unlined. She hardly recognized him like that, so happy and lighthearted, as if he were king of the whole, wide world.

Pain clutching her heart, she turned the page. More family pictures. Laura and Clare. McBride and Clare. All three of them at the beach, in the kitchen, in front of a Christmas tree. Clare alone, grinning at the camera, her face smeared with what looked like strained carrots. Lily laughed and cried at the sweet, funny little face.

With each successive photo, Lily watched Clare grow. First a crawling baby, then a wobbly toddler, then a sassy two-year-old. The very last picture in the album was another eight-by-ten portrait. It was Clare at age three. Probably the last photograph McBride had of his daughter, Lily realized.

She studied the picture, looked at every inch of the little girl's face, trying to commit her to memory. Clare had her mother's fair skin and quaint heart-shaped face. Her daddy's dark hazel eyes.

Lily's heart flip-flopped. Her fingers tightened on the album and she drew a sharp breath.

That face.

She'd seen it, leaner and sadder, without the little-girl chubbiness. She'd seen those hazel eyes, no longer sparkling with childlike wonder, but serious and worried. Lily plucked at the peel-away covering holding the photo in place and pulled it free from the sticky backing, managing not to damage the picture. Her hands shook as she flipped the photo over to see if anything was written on the back.

"Katherine Clare McBride, age three."

Katherine Clare.

Not Casey, Lily realized.

K.C.

She released a shuddering breath, afraid to move. She

remembered the little girl's words. "Daddy calls me Casey."

Daddy calls me K.C.

Casey was Clare McBride.

Chapter Sixteen

McBride turned to look at her. His gaze dropped to the album in her hands. A dozen different expressions flitted over his face before he finally settled on a sort of sad acceptance. "That's Clare."

Lily's chest tightened, afraid that what she was about to tell him would be more than he could take. "She's beautiful."

"Is it horrible that when I saw Andrew Walters run to his little girl, all I could think was, I wish that was me?" McBride sat down at the table beside her, taking the photo from her hands. He ran his fingers over it and looked up at her. "I wish you could have found Clare for me."

When Lily reached out to touch his face, her hand was shaking. "What if I told you I could?"

"Find Clare?"

"Yes."

He looked puzzled. "Why are you asking this?"

Her stomach clenched. "Would you believe me?"

"Is this some kind of test?"

Lily shook her head. "I just need to know."

Silence stretched between them for a long moment.

Lily's tension rose to the snapping point before he finally spoke. "If you looked me in the face and told me you knew where Clare was, yes, I'd believe you." In his murky eyes she saw a depth of desperation she'd never seen before. "I'd give my soul to believe Clare was still alive."

She lowered her trembling hand and asked the question she dreaded most. But it had to be asked, because there was always a chance she was wrong about who Casey really was. "What if I told you I could find Clare, but it turned out I couldn't?"

McBride's face shut down as if somebody had turned off the lights. Lily had her answer before he said the words. "I think I'd hate you the rest of my life."

The coldness of McBride's reply gave her chills. Her trembling increased, vibrations rolling along her spine.

Gray mist began to swirl.

The door in her mind banged open and she heard her name as clearly as if someone had called to her across the room.

"Help me, Lily!" Casey's pale face appeared in the mist. She held out her arms.

Without a second thought, Lily went to her. The mist dissipated, revealing Casey's bedroom. Lily gently lifted the little girl's face. "Are you hurt?"

"Mama locked me in here and she won't let me out and I can't hear anything. I'm hungry and I'm scared and I need to pee. Please, Lily, help me, please!" Tears streamed down Casey's face. "Please, Lily, I'm scared!"

"Shh, sweetie, it's okay. I'm here and I'll help you, okay? But I need you to calm down and help me, too."

Casey made a visible effort to calm herself, rubbing her tear-reddened eyes. "Okay."

"Your mother locked the door and you can't get it open?"

"No, I can't."

"Show me."

Casey went over and tried to turn the doorknob. Lily heard the rattle as it refused to move. For some reason Lily didn't want to think about too closely, the door locked from the outside. "Casey, how was your mother acting?"

"She kept yelling at me to stop screaming, but I wasn't, Lily. Honest, I wasn't screaming at all."

The woman must have been having a psychotic episode, Lily thought with trepidation. Casey might be safer locked in her room for now. But how long until the woman came back?

Lily scanned her surroundings for anything that could help the child escape. "What about the window?"

"I can't open it."

"Try it for me again." Maybe it was just stuck.

Casey moved toward the window. The sill was only a couple of feet off the floor, so Casey had no trouble gripping the handles and giving the window a jerk. But it wouldn't budge.

Out the window, Lily saw a short stretch of unkempt grass before the surrounding woods took over. The window was low enough to the ground that Casey could climb out, if they could ever get it open. "Casey, I need to come to where you are. Do you know the name of your town?"

She shook her head. "Mama never lets me leave here. I can only go to the edge of the woods."

Lily frowned. "You don't go to school?"

Casey shook her head. "But I know how to read. Mama taught me, before she got so sick."

Lily sensed the child wasn't far away; the woods and general terrain looked familiar. "Are you in Alabama?"

"Yes!" Excitement shone in Casey's eyes. "Mama taught me a song. 'My home's in Alabama, no matter where—'"

A sharp crack interrupted Casey's slightly off-key rendition. Her eyes widened. "What was that?"

Lily stared back, her heart racing. She feared she knew exactly what that sound had been.

A gunshot.

MCBRIDE SAID LILY'S NAME. She didn't respond.

A chill ran down his spine as he sat back from her, unsure what to do. A few moments ago, she'd just…left. Her eyes had gone glassy, her face flushed, and then she was gone to wherever it was she went when one of her visions hit.

Was it what he'd told her? He hadn't meant to be so harsh, but she'd said she wanted the truth. He didn't know if he could ever forgive her if she convinced him once more that Clare might still be alive, only to fail to deliver on her promise.

But it was a moot point, wasn't it? He'd accepted a long time ago that his little girl was dead.

McBride touched Lily's face, wondering if it was bad for her to have her visions interrupted. Would it give her one of those horrible migraines? He didn't know how it worked.

"No!" An anguished wail poured forth from deep inside Lily, setting McBride's teeth on edge.

Suddenly, her eyes blinked rapidly and focused, then widened in alarm. She gripped his arms. "McBride, we've got to find her!"

She was still having visions of Abby? "We've already found her, Lily. Abby's safe with her daddy."

"Not Abby!" Lily clutched his shoulders and pulled herself to her feet. "Clare's in trouble. We have to help her!"

Blood roared in McBride's ears. "Clare?"

Lily's gaze pierced his heart. Her lips moved soundlessly for a moment, as if she were searching desperately for words. Then her voice broke through, raspy and quivering. "She's alive, McBride. Clare's alive."

He felt the blood drain from his head. "No."

"She's alive and she needs our help." Lily touched his face, her fingers hot and dry. "I know you're afraid to believe, but we don't have time."

He pushed her hand away. "Lily, don't do this."

"You said you'd believe me if I told you I knew where she was. I know the risk I'm taking." She grabbed his chin and forced him to look into her eyes. "I know it can destroy us."

He swallowed hard. "You saw her just now?"

"She's the little girl I told you about." Lily pointed to Clare's photo. "This is her. Only she's older—nine or ten."

His body went numb. "But she said her name was Casey."

"K.C., McBride. Katherine Clare. You called her K.C., didn't you?"

He gazed at Lily, his heart in his throat. "We called her Clare, after her aunt Clare. But sometimes I called her K.C."

"It's your daughter, McBride. She's not dead."

Tears filled his eyes. He slowly lifted his hands to his face. "Not dead."

"She's in trouble. We have to find her."

He looked up, a fresh agony of despair rolling over him. "How? You don't know where she is."

Lily told him everything she'd seen of Casey in her visions—the old-fashioned parlor, the small bedroom, the distant and disturbed woman Casey called Mama. "Does it ring any bells with you at all?"

"Maybe she just looks like Clare." He wobbled on the edge of belief, afraid to take the final plunge.

Lily released a sigh of pure frustration. "There has to be something..." Her eyes suddenly lit up. "You gave her a stuffed frog. Mr. Green. You said he'd watch out for her."

McBride's heart skipped a beat, then hurtled into hyperspeed. He could see the green frog as clearly as if he'd bought it just the day before.

Doubt left him, washed away in a bittersweet flood of hope.

Casey was his daughter, Clare. And Lily was going to help him find her.

PARFAIT-PINK WALLS, cracked in places and peeling...

It took Lily a few moments to realize she was seeing the morning sun reflected off the dingy walls of Casey's tiny bedroom instead of McBride's kitchen. Panic clawed her insides. Where was the girl? Had the madwoman done something to her?

"I'm here." Casey crouched in the corner, clutching her toy frog.

"Why are you on the floor?" Lily asked.

Casey waved at the bed. Lily saw that the sheets were wadded into a ball in the middle of the lumpy mattress. She smelled something sour.

"I couldn't hold it." Casey sniffled. "I tried to find something to use, but I couldn't hold it anymore."

Lily crossed to her quickly, stroking Casey's face. "It's okay. Your daddy and I are going to get you out of here."

"Daddy?"

Lily smiled at the sudden rush of hope she saw in Casey's face. "Your daddy's with me right now, honey. He never wanted to let you go. Nobody gave him a choice. But I told him about you. We're going to help you, but you have to help us do it."

Casey nodded eagerly. "How?"

"I want you to put on warm clothes. Do you have warm clothes in this room?"

"Yes." Casey rose quickly and started rummaging through the battered chest of drawers near the window. She donned fresh underclothes, a pair of jeans and a too-snug sweater.

"Put on another sweater, and at least two pairs of socks," Lily directed, at the same time trying to listen for any noises from outside the room.

Casey did as she said.

"Now, wrap that other pair of blue jeans around your arm and hit the window as hard as you can."

Casey's eyes widened. "What if Mama hears?"

Lily didn't know what to say. She wasn't sure if the woman was even alive anymore. Or if she was, maybe she was too far gone to hear anything, lost in the depths of another catatonic episode. Lily almost hoped so. If the woman were to come into this room and do something to Casey while Lily was there watching…

She shuddered, feeling the door in her mind trying to open and pull her back to reality. She clenched her teeth and fought it like a mother tiger. Concentrating on Casey, she was able to stay in the vision, but already her head was beginning to ache.

"Hit it, Casey."

Casey planted her feet in front of the window and took a deep breath. Lily could see her nibbling her bottom lip in preparation. At that moment, she looked just like McBride.

Then she struck the window with her padded hand. The glass rattled but didn't give.

They both waited a few seconds, breaths bated, listening for any noise from outside the room.

Nothing.

"Hit it again," Lily said.

Casey slammed her hand into the window. This time, one pane broke, sending shards flying.

"Again, Casey!"

The girl banged the windowpane next to the broken one. It shattered as well. She hit each pane with increasing force, smashing them until the bottom six panes were broken.

"Now, Casey, here's the hard part. Strike the wooden part as hard as you can. Strike it until it breaks."

The little girl made a soft growling noise deep in her throat, then started hammering away at the wood. Pieces splintered outward bit by bit until she'd made a space large enough to crawl through. Lily felt the biting cold October air pouring through the opening.

She told Casey to drape more clothing over the ragged places to protect herself. Then the girl crawled through the opening and tumbled to the ground.

Lily envisioned herself following through the window,

and she was suddenly outside, where Casey was picking herself up and dusting off her jeans. Sunlight pierced the wall of trees in the east, washing everything in gold. The child started running toward the sunlight and Lily tried to follow, but her throbbing head slowed her. "Wait, Casey! Where are you going?"

Lily felt the door in her mind opening, drawing her back. Desperately, she looked around, trying to memorize every detail. The one-story house, white paint with green shutters. Sagging gutters. Unkempt yard. Trees all around.

Then she saw the spire. It rose against the eastern sky, little more than a dark silhouette just above the treetops, but she thought it might be a church steeple.

She kept her eyes on the spire until the mists surrounded her, dragging her back to her own time and place.

Lily jerked in her chair, nearly toppling over. "McBride!"

He was right beside her. "What is it?"

She grabbed his arm. "I saw her! She's out of the house, and I think I know how we can find her!"

He caught her shoulders. "What did you see?"

He made her go over everything she'd experienced, sifting the facts carefully, looking for hidden clues. She gritted her teeth against the pain in her head and told him everything she could remember. He latched on to the spire, of course. It was probably the best clue they had.

"It was like a church steeple," she said. "I couldn't see it all that well, but what else could it be?"

"Okay, let's look at what we've got." He pulled a notebook from the kitchen counter and wrote as he spoke. "The house is in a small clearing. It's one-story, white with green shutters. The gutters are sagging and it looks to be isolated. The back of the house faces what direction?"

She closed her eyes, fighting pain as she tried to picture the scene that had played out before her eyes. "South."

"Okay, the front faces north, then. And the church spire is in the east…" His voice trailed off suddenly. She looked at him, and found his eyes wide.

"What is it?"

"I think I know where that church is!" His voice shook with excitement. "It's in the middle of the woods, like you said. If I find the church, I can backtrack to the house." He kissed her quickly and started toward the bedroom.

"Wait, I'm coming with you." She tried to stand, but her head swam. She stumbled into the table.

He was at her side in a second, arms circling her. He caught her chin in his hand and lifted her face to his. "Did you fight the vision?" he asked, looking surprised.

"It was trying to bring me back before I was ready. I wouldn't let it."

"Are your pills in your purse?"

"I'll get them. You go."

"I'll be back soon." Brushing her hair aside, he kissed her forehead. "How will I ever be able to thank you for this?"

She caught his hands. "Just bring Clare home."

THE GRAVEL ROAD LED to the Barclay United Methodist Church, a small white clapboard building in the middle of Barclay Woods. McBride parked the car and got out, staring at the tall steeple. His heart banged against the back of his throat as he looked toward the spot where the spire seemed to prick the veil of heaven.

She's here somewhere, isn't she?

He closed his eyes and opened his heart, calling to his

little girl with every ounce of love he had inside him. *Daddy loves you, K.C., he loves you so much.*

He called her name aloud. "K.C.!"

The sound echoed in the early morning quiet of the woods. Only the soft chirping of birds and the chatter of squirrels answered him.

God, please don't let this happen again.

"K.C.?"

The silence compelled him forward, into the forest. He jogged through the tangled underbrush, sometimes stumbling, sometimes sliding, always moving west toward the house he knew had to be just beyond the next stand of trees. He called his daughter's name as he ran, his voice ragged and shaking.

When he saw the edge of a clearing through the wall of trees, he staggered to a halt. The sound of his breathing was harsh in the stillness. He took a step forward, then another. His strides sped up and he finally broke into the clearing, where he halted again and stared.

There it was, just as Lily had said. A small, one-story white house with green shutters. Overgrown grass, sagging roof.

This was it! She was right.

Hope surged through him like new blood, propelling him forward. He ran around the side of the house, heedless of any possible danger, his heart, mind and soul set on one goal: finding his daughter. He turned the corner and ran a few steps more before his feet caught up with his eyes.

The silence swallowed him whole.

Bile coursed upward through his esophagus, gagging him. Squeezing his eyes shut, he turned his head and retched, falling to his hands and knees. Ice seemed to replace his blood as his stomach emptied, leaving him stiff and cold.

Finally, he stopped retching and found the strength to turn his head again, clinging to one last sliver of hope. Maybe adrenaline had played tricks on him. Maybe he'd been so afraid of having his hopes dashed again that he'd created his own worst nightmare.

He slowly opened his eyes. His heart sank.

The entire front of the place was a blackened ruin, gutted by a fire long since extinguished. This house hadn't been occupied in years.

McBride hung his head, wishing he were dead.

LILY SLEPT FITFULLY, dark dreams disturbing her slumber. She was in a black space, blacker than night, blacker than death, and she could hear McBride calling his daughter's name.

"K.C.!"

The sound echoed in her head, a hard, brittle noise. It sounded like blood tasted, she realized. Sharp and metallic.

"Liar!"

She twitched in her sleep as McBride's voice stabbed her in the heart.

"You said she was alive! You said I could find her, but you were wrong!"

She ran from the malignant thickness of that voice, crying as she ran. Her tears were acid, burning her cheeks. She couldn't escape the fiery heat of McBride's hatred.

"I hate you for what you've done!" McBride's voice pursued her in her nightmare.

Lily jerked awake with a cry, clawing at the bedcovers

that held her prisoner. Her heart caught as she realized McBride was sitting in a chair next to the bed, looking at her with eyes as dead as winter.

"Oh, God." Lily choked on the words.

He looked away from her.

"You didn't find her." Her heart plummeted.

McBride didn't glance at her again. "You're right. She wasn't there."

"Did you find the church?"

"Yeah. I even found the house. But Clare wasn't there."

"You mean you didn't find her at the house." Lily felt a glimmer of hope. "McBride, I told you that she ran away. She was probably out in the woods, hiding. If we just go back, I'm sure—"

"No." McBride's voice sounded hollow. "I found the house. Dirty white with green shutters, sagging roof—everything was just right. But it was gutted by fire a long time ago. Nobody's lived in that house in years."

Lily shook her head. How could that be? "But Abby saw her, too."

"You were in Abby's head, Lily. She probably saw whatever you saw."

"Why would I see your daughter if she wasn't there? Before yesterday I didn't even know you had a daughter. And I didn't see a three-year-old. This was a grown-up nine-year-old." Lily shook her head. "Maybe we were wrong about where the house was in relation to the church. Or maybe we had the wrong house."

"Stop!" He doubled over as if in pain. "Please, just stop, Lily. I can't do this anymore."

But I wasn't wrong about Abby, she thought, desperately clinging to that fact. Abby had been right there where she'd seen her. She couldn't understand why McBride hadn't found K.C. "I don't know what happened. After we found Abby, I was so sure…" Hot tears sprang to her eyes.

"I'm not saying you don't have some kind of ability," McBride said. "Finding Abby was proof of that. But you were obviously wrong about Clare."

The one failure he'd never be able to forgive. He'd said as much. Tears trickled down Lily's cheeks. "I'm so sorry, McBride."

He nodded, but he still didn't look at her. "I know you believed you had found Clare. It's really not your fault." He rubbed his jaw. "It's my fault. I knew better than to let myself believe again. I knew all the risks, what it was going to cost me, but I did it anyway. I should've known better."

The pain in her head had faded, but her heart was ripping apart. "You want me to leave."

He didn't answer for a few seconds, and she almost dared to hope. But then he nodded slowly. "I know I'm not being fair to you. But I know now that I can't do this. I've called Theo to follow you home. He's waiting outside."

She could tell by the sound of his voice that she'd never be able to convince him otherwise.

Tamping down despair, she stood, legs wobbling as she crossed in front of him, barely able to keep her hands from reaching out to touch him. She went to the closet, where she'd put some of the clothes from her overnight bag.

"I'll do that," he said. "Your head's still hurting."

She leaned against the frame of the closet door, her chest aching with pent-up grief. She had known the risks as well. She'd known that trying to find Casey could cost her the chance of being with McBride.

But she'd been so sure.

How could she have been so wrong about Casey when she'd been so right about Abby? Lily just didn't know how the visions worked. She didn't know what caused them, how to control them or what they meant. It had been arrogant to think she did.

She pushed herself upright and turned to McBride. He stood near the dresser, folding her clothes and putting them into the overnight bag. He avoided looking at her, as if the sight of her was more than he could bear.

She sought the strength to ask him one hard, dreaded question. "Did you ever love me, McBride? Even a little?"

A muscle in his jaw jumped. He turned and looked at her, his gaze cold, his expression nearly blank. "I just knew I was going to find her today. I thought I could feel her with me. It was like I could reach out my hand and touch her. And I thought, Lily did this for me. She brought my baby back to me."

Lily gritted her teeth, holding back a sob.

McBride shut his eyes. "Then I found that burned-out house." His shoulders rose and fell with a deep sigh. "You want to know how I feel about you? I don't feel anything, Lily. I just don't…feel." He turned away, pulling out the dresser drawer where she'd put some of her belongings.

Unable to find anything else to say, Lily joined him by the dresser and started putting her clothes into the overnight bag. They moved in slow, silent concert, methodically erasing all evidence that she'd ever been part of his life.

She closed the case, and McBride took it from her, heading toward the hallway. He walked her out to her rental car, pausing as she slid behind the wheel. "You'll probably want to get out of town for a while," he said. "I'll take care of it with Brody. There'll be reporters hunting you down if you hang around."

She looked at him, studied him one last time. She wished she had a photo, some memento she could pull out when the nights were long and lonely. Something to remember him by. But they hadn't been together long enough for love notes, dried roses or any of the forget-me-nots that accompanied lost love.

All she would have was the memory of this moment to haunt her for a lifetime.

McBride waved at Theo Baker who sat behind the wheel of a dark sedan idling at the curb. Then he finally looked at her one last time, his dark gaze unfathomable. After a moment, he turned and started walking back to the house.

She slumped in the driver's seat and shut her eyes, aching with misery. Casey had been so real to her. She could still see her little face, still hear her voice in her head.

What if she was really out there somewhere? Maybe not McBride's daughter, Clare, but somebody, some scared little girl, lost and all by herself?

Lily didn't know. She didn't know if finding Abby had been a fluke, a once-in-a-lifetime lucky break. She didn't know if her gift was reliable. She didn't even know if there ever was a little girl named Casey who was hiding in the woods, waiting for her daddy and Lily to come rescue her.

She didn't know anything anymore.

Chapter Seventeen

When Lily arrived home a little after ten, Agent Logan stood on her front stoop talking to a dark-haired man with a bushy mustache. The sketch artist McBride had called, she realized, spotting the sketch pad under the stranger's arm. She'd forgotten all about the meeting.

Agent Logan smiled in greeting. "I'll be down the street if you need me, Ms. Browning." He headed down the driveway, stopping briefly to speak to Theo Baker.

The mustached man introduced himself as Jim Phillips. Waving off her offer of something to drink, he went right to work, listening to her description of the man she'd seen in the woods. His charcoal pencil flew across the paper as she viewed the results and helped him tweak the sketch.

Within a half hour, he'd managed to draw a very good likeness of the man she'd seen following Abby.

"That's him," she finally declared.

Jim closed the sketch pad and shook her hand. "Thanks for the input—you have a good eye. I'll be sure McBride gets this ASAP."

His mention of McBride felt like a stab in the heart, but she kept her chin up until she'd ushered him out the door.

She glanced down the street, looking for the FBI van. It was no longer where it had been parked earlier. A niggle of unease tickled her spine, but she pushed it away. They were probably hidden from plain view. The FBI was good at that, she'd heard.

Still, she thought as she closed the door, she'd feel safer if she could see them.

Slumping on her sofa, she tried to coax her cats to her lap, but they kept their distance, glaring at her from the doorway. "It was overnight, not a week," she protested. "I left you plenty of food and water."

They didn't budge from the doorway, gazing at her with pure feline disdain. Lily gave up and sat back, closing her eyes.

A knock on her front door jerked her upright, nerves jangling. Her cats scattered.

McBride, she thought, her heart leaping with hope.

But it was Andrew Walters who stood on her doorstep.

CAL BRODY WAS WAITING for McBride when he arrived at the station. The agent took his own sweet time vacating McBride's desk chair, which only darkened McBride's already pitch-black mood. But he welcomed the rush of anger. After the past couple of hours, it was good to feel anything, even rage.

"I've gone over the evidence retrieval in this case, and I've got to hand it to you, Lieutenant, it's damn good," Brody commented. "You've got good people here."

"Did you think this was Hooterville or something? Of course we did a good job." McBride glared at him.

"Didn't mean any offense." Brody quirked his thick, dark brows. "Your captain has refused further FBI assistance in investigating the deaths of the two kidnappers, and we've already found forensic evidence that Rick 'Skeet' Scotero killed Debra Walters. So we're done here. We're heading back to Birmingham."

McBride's brow furrowed. "What about your surveillance unit at Lily Browning's house?"

"We packed them up an hour ago. She's not a witness, and we're pretty sure that the men who called her are dead." Brody's eyes narrowed. "Unless you want us to continue investigating her as a possible accomplice?"

McBride's patience snapped. "Oh, for God's sake, Brody. She's not a suspect. You know it. I know it. Now get out of my office so I can get some work done."

"By the way, Walters called to say thanks again." Brody actually smiled, although the expression looked strange on him. "Nice that at least part of this mess ended well."

After Brody left, McBride passed his hand over his face, feeling sick. He didn't want to think about Andrew Walters with his beautiful, healthy little girl, while McBride was sitting here, wondering why he had to keep going through hell over and over again, losing everyone and everything that gave meaning to his life.

He grabbed his bottle of antacid tablets and twisted open the top. He crunched two tablets, unsure if they'd be strong enough to calm the acid bath churning in his gut. Reaching for his phone, he arranged for a patrol unit to watch Lily Browning until he could figure out what to do with her next.

No matter how much he was hurting right now, letting her go home alone had been damn near a dereliction of duty.

"HOW'D YOU MANAGE to evade the reporters?" Lily asked as she settled in the armchair across from Andrew Walters.

"I'm used to it by now. I've learned the tricks." Andrew stretched one arm across the back of her sofa. "Abby sends her love. She's with my ex-wife's sister in Tellerville."

"I'm sorry I didn't get to say goodbye." Lily tamped down her disappointment. "But I'm so happy she's safe."

"Thanks to you." Andrew leaned forward. "I'm hoping you can answer something for me. Abby keeps talking about someone named Casey. Do you know who she's talking about?"

Tears stung the back of Lily's eyes. "She's a little girl who showed up in some of my visions of Abby."

"Showed up?"

"She wasn't physically there in the trailer with Abby. She just…appeared."

"Appeared? How?"

"I think maybe she's clairvoyant, too."

Andrew shook his head, his lips curving in a half smile. "This is all so…"

"Weird?" Lily supplied.

He nodded. "Abby says Casey's the one who told her about the man with the gun."

Remembering McBride's warning, Lily played dumb. "What man with a gun?"

"I believe it must be the man who killed the two men who took Abby. Abby said he was following her in the woods."

Lily feigned surprise. "I heard the men were dead, but…"

"The FBI think it may have something to do with the senate race." Andrew's expression oozed dismay, but he couldn't hide a tiny glimmer of satisfaction in his blue eyes. Anything that cast doubt on his opponent would aid his bid to become the next senator from Alabama, Lily realized. That was politics.

"Horrible," she murmured, not really sure what else to say.

"So you never saw the kidnappers or anyone else in your visions? Just Abby?"

"Just Abby," she lied. "And Casey, of course."

"What does Casey look like?"

Lily's stomach tightened. "She's just a little girl," she said, being deliberately vague. "A little older than your daughter. I didn't see that much of her. I was more focused on Abby."

"I see." He sounded disappointed. "I'd have liked to thank her, too. Abby said Casey was a great source of comfort."

"I don't think I'll be seeing any more of her." Lily's throat tightened with misery. Andrew's questions only reminded her of all she'd lost.

A shudder ran down her back, sprinkling gooseflesh across her arms and legs. Another shiver washed over her, giving her less than a second's notice before the vision slammed open the door in her mind and pulled her inside.

The gray mist dissipated with shocking suddenness, and Lily almost tripped over Casey. The little girl was huddled in a dark place, hands tucked into the sleeves of her sweater. She was shivering, but her color looked good, Lily noted with a rush of relief. She said Casey's name.

The little girl's dark hazel eyes lifted. She scrambled to her feet. "Lily, I thought you'd gone away forever!"

Lily wrapped her arms around the child and hugged her tightly, tears streaming down her face. "It's okay, Casey. I found you."

MCBRIDE HEARD FROM the patrolmen he'd sent to check on Lily just before eleven. "Andrew Walters arrived a few minutes ago, and Ms. Browning let him in," the officer related. "Want us to stand by?"

"Stay a little up the street," McBride ordered. He didn't want Lily to feel like a suspect.

He hung up the phone and tried to finish some paperwork. But minutes later, he pushed aside his keyboard and admitted what he'd been avoiding since Lily walked out his door.

He loved her.

He didn't want to love her. His life would be less painful and less scary if he didn't feel anything for her. He had pushed her away, let himself blame her for his pain, but she refused to leave his heart.

Now he knew she never would.

Loving her made him question his own skepticism, the hard, cold anger he'd carried inside him after Clare disappeared, even his treatment of Delaine Howard, a woman who'd only been trying to help him. Maybe she'd given them false hope about Clare when caution would've been kinder, but she'd tried to help, just as Lily had. That counted for something.

In Lily's case, it counted for everything.

She had been right about Abby Walters. No way to deny that; the little girl was living proof. Yet Lily had been so wrong about Clare.

McBride rubbed his burning eyes. Okay. She had made a mistake in identifying the little girl. But he didn't think she'd invented the story of Casey.

So if she wasn't Clare, who was she?

The door to his office opened and Theo Baker entered, his eyebrows nearly meeting his hairline. In his wake strode Senator Gerald Blackledge and his security detail. "The senator would like a word with us," Baker said.

Blackledge didn't wait for an invitation to sit. He laid a manila folder on McBride's desk and dropped into the chair across from him. "I realize your case just got a whole lot harder for you, so I'm here to simplify things a little bit."

McBride opened the folder and found page after page of polling data. "This simplifies things?"

"Look at the dates and the polls. Those are my campaign's internals, notarized by the independent polling firm we hired to gather the information. They will be willing to testify to the time and date stamps and the veracity of the information."

McBride scanned the pages, checking the notary marks as well as the dates, before he went back to look at what the polls revealed. He had to go over them twice to be sure he understood what he was seeing. "You were pulling way ahead."

"Exactly," Blackledge said with a nod. "We knew that three weeks ago. Why on God's green earth would I try to put Andrew Walters's name back on the front page of the newspaper, especially in such a sympathetic light?"

He wouldn't, McBride realized. The notarized polling data erased what nebulous motive he might have. "I'll be following up with your polling company."

"I'd expect no less." Blackledge stood and motioned for his entourage to follow him out.

"Wait a second, Senator." McBride crossed to the doorway. "Do you think the Walters's campaign had the same polling information?"

Blackledge's brown eyes glittered. "I would think so."

McBride watched the senator leave, his own eyes narrowed.

"If Walters knew about those polls…" Baker began.

Before he could finish, Jim Phillips stuck his head through the open doorway. "Got a minute for me, McBride?"

McBride cocked his head. He'd forgotten about sending the sketch artist. "Did you see Ms. Browning this morning?"

"I did." Jim handed McBride his sketch pad. "She's got a good eye for detail."

McBride gazed down at the sketch, taking in the sandy hair, fleshy features and prominent forehead of the man in the sketch. Recognition dawned, followed quickly by a flood of cold dread.

Son of a bitch.

IGNORING THE GRAY MIST curling closer, beckoning her back to reality, Lily started looking around her, seeking some clue to Casey's whereabouts. The room was dark and dusty, pierced in places by slivers of light peeking through cracks in the walls and clean patches in the filthy windows. She couldn't make out many details, but the setup was unmistakable. Casey was in an old, abandoned schoolhouse.

"Casey, tell me everything you can remember about how you got here. Did you notice any landmarks, anything unusual?"

Casey shook her head. "It was just woods, lots of pines and dead trees. I saw squirrels and birds—wait!" Her eyes brightened. "I had to cross a stream! I was so proud 'cause I got across on the rocks without getting my feet wet."

That might be a help if Lily could narrow down the possibilities. But there had to be dozens of old, abandoned schoolhouses in Alabama. She glanced about, seeking something that could tell her for certain where the child was. "Casey, help me look around. See if you can find anything that has a name written on it. Look in the desks."

Casey crossed to the nearest desk and opened the top. She jumped and squealed when a spider darted across her hand, but quickly shook it off and started searching through the yellowed papers. Lily peered through the gloom but could make out none of the faded words. "Try the next one."

In the fifth desk they hit pay dirt. There was an old primer with a faded blue stamp in front. "Willow Wood School," Casey read aloud.

Not ten miles away, Lily realized with wonder.

She grabbed the girl and hugged her tightly. The fog thickened around her. "I know where you are, baby," she told Casey as the mist began to separate them. "I'll be there soon, I promise."

She came back to herself in a rush.

"My God, Lily, are you okay?"

She blinked, surprised to find herself in her living room, sitting across from Andrew Walters.

"What just happened? Did you have a vision?"

She pushed herself to her feet, her knees wobbly. "Andrew, I'm sorry—I have to go. I'll be in touch, I promise."

He followed her to her car. "Are you sure you're okay to drive? I can take you wherever—"

"I'm fine." She slid behind the wheel and started the engine with shaking hands, backing down the drive and out onto the street with reckless speed, racing time and her pounding heart to get to McBride's daughter.

HE KEPT HIS EYES ON Lily Browning's rental car, forcing down the panic rising like a gusher in his throat. She'd seen him. And so had some kid named Casey.

Who the hell was she? How had she seen him?

He kept pace with Lily as she raced down the street, but didn't get too close. He couldn't risk spooking her before she led him to wherever the little girl was hiding. *Please, let her take me there!*

Then he could finally tie up the last loose end.

"I'm not going down for this. This was your idea."

He ignored the pale-faced man next to him. They'd come up with the plan together and they would finish it together.

"What if she's not going after the kid?"

"She is," he growled.

She had to be.

She'd seen him in the woods, while she was helping Abby get to safety. She and the kid named Casey. They were the only ones who could bring the whole mess crashing down on his head.

They had to be stopped.

MCBRIDE GRITTED HIS TEETH with frustration at the sea of red taillights forming about two miles down the interstate. Flashing blue and cherry lights in the distance marked the site of the accident that appeared to be snarling traffic.

He didn't want to wait. He had to get to Lily now.

Between McBride and the sea of taillights ahead was an exit onto Boudreau Road. It was probably fifteen minutes out of his way, but the interstate traffic would take at least that long to clear. Yanking the wheel to the right, he headed for the exit.

Boudreau Road stretched for six miles through beautiful, wild terrain thick with towering green pines and hardwoods already changing colors and losing their leaves.

His stomach ached. It looked like the road he'd traveled on his way to the church in Barclay Woods.

Just beyond the bridge over Tuttle Creek, the road began winding downhill, giving McBride a panoramic view of the valley beyond.

His breath caught.

Just a mile or two ahead, glistening in the midday sunlight, a white spire rose above the pines.

He heard Lily's voice in his mind. *It was like a church steeple. I couldn't see it well, but what else could it be?*

A schoolhouse, he thought, gazing at the bell tower. It could be a schoolhouse.

The car shimmied as he pulled off the road. His heart pounded wildly in his chest. It couldn't be. Could it?

He took a second to get his bearings. It was after noon now, so the sun was inching toward the western sky. Best he could tell, he was due west of the tower. If Lily had been right, there was probably a road to his left.

Of course, that was a big if. But he had to know.

He drove another half mile before he caught sight of a side road winding into the woods. He braked quickly, almost skidding, and turned down the dirt road. He had gone about twenty yards when his mind registered the mailbox that had been directly across from the turnoff.

McBride backed to the edge of the pavement, jerked the car into Park and got out. He walked back to the roadside and looked across the blacktop at the rusted mailbox. Corroded brass numbers climbed the wooden post, hanging askew. Stick-on letters on the box spelled out one name: Grainger.

McBride drew a swift breath, chill bumps breaking out on his arms and back.

This was the mailbox Delaine Howard had seen in her vision all those years ago. *This* Grainger.

This is it, he realized, his pulse thudding in his ears.

He raced back to the car.

The road became almost unnavigable the deeper he went into the woods. He clenched his teeth and wrestled with the steering wheel, holding the Chevy on the bumpy dirt drive. When he was almost ready to park the car and walk the rest of the way, the road smoothed out and he saw the edge of a clearing just ahead.

Stifling the urge to gun the engine, he drove on. Now he could see a white building peeking through the trees.

A white clapboard house with faded green shutters.

Clearing the edge of the woods, he pulled into the high grass behind the house. His whole body clenched as he cut the engine and got out. He hesitated, struck by how similar this house looked to the one he'd come across just this morning. The shape was different, the green paint on the shutters darker. But it matched the general description Lily had given.

He looked to his right. Above the trees, lit by the bright sun, loomed the top of the schoolhouse bell tower.

This is what Lily saw, he thought. He took a deep, bracing breath and walked slowly through the high grass, rounding the corner of the house. He was half prepared to find another burned-out shell. But the house was intact.

He pulled open the shabby, ripped screen door and

knocked. There was no answer, so he knocked again. Still no answer. He tried the doorknob and was surprised when it turned easily in his hand. "Hello?"

Then the smell hit him. Sharp. Metallic.

Blood.

His heart hammered as he pulled his Smith & Wesson from his shoulder holster and rushed inside. He was being reckless as hell, but fear eclipsed reason as he remembered the gunshot Lily said she'd heard in her vision.

Had the woman done something to his baby girl?

He burst through the kitchen doorway into the hall and almost slipped as his feet hit a sticky wet patch. He grabbed the doorjamb and stared at the dark pool of blood at his feet.

Just in front of him lay the body of a woman.

The cop in him took over for a second, surveying the scene with clinical detachment. Head shot, probably instantly fatal. From the looks of the scene, self-inflicted.

Then his heart overcame the initial numbness and he darted past the body, heedless of how he was compromising the crime scene. He tried each door down the hall. At the very end on the left, he found a locked one.

He hit the door with several sharp shoulder blows, ignoring the pain. The wood finally splintered and he burst inside.

It was a child's bedroom. It fit Lily's description, right down to the broken window.

Clare's alive, he realized, his heart in his throat.

He raced back down the hall, past the body and out the door. He ran past the car and plunged into the woods, keeping his eyes on the schoolhouse bell tower.

LILY PULLED OFF THE ROAD onto a dirt track leading into the woods. The uneven terrain put the rental's shocks to the test, jostling her around despite the seat belt holding her in place. She went as far as the road would take her and finally pulled over, heading the rest of the way on foot. The woods were thick with underbrush, making the path to the old schoolhouse hard to travel, but Lily crashed ahead, heedless of the twigs and vines that slapped against her legs as she ran.

She made enough noise that she almost didn't hear the rustling underbrush behind her.

Almost.

A finger of fear sketched a cold path up her spine. She darted to her right, taking cover behind a thick-trunked pine. Heart pounding, she took a quick peek at the woods behind her.

A sandy-haired man pushed through the heavy underbrush, a large pistol in one hand. And next to him, brow furrowed with determination, walked Andrew Walters.

Chapter Eighteen

McBride raced through the woods, calling his daughter's name until he was hoarse. It was taking longer than he'd expected to reach the schoolhouse, but he didn't want to risk missing Clare hidden behind a bush or tangle in the thick underbrush. Within minutes, he was close enough to see the shabby white clapboard building peeking through the tree trunks as the woods thinned out. He started jogging toward the building, something unseen but powerful tugging at his heart.

He burst into the clearing and stared at the schoolhouse. It was dingy white, set about four feet off the ground on a natural stone foundation. Sagging pine steps led to a narrow porch in front of the double doors. McBride saw the door was open a crack. "Clare?"

He stood very still, listening. His heart lurched at a faint rustling sound coming from inside. He tried to temper the surge of adrenaline, reminding himself the noise could be a squirrel or a bird trapped in the building.

But deep inside, he knew.

"K.C.!" he called. "K.C., it's Daddy!"

He heard the soft rustle again. His heart banged against

his ribs as he stared into the gloom beyond the partially opened door. He wanted to dash up the stairs but feared they wouldn't bear his weight. He stopped at the bottom and peered into the darkness. "K.C.?"

A small oval face seemed to materialize from the darkness inside. McBride took a swift, shuddering breath.

A dark-haired wraith emerged from the schoolhouse, her hazel eyes huge in her pale, heart-shaped face. McBride sank to his knees, his mind whirling.

"Daddy?" Her voice was faint.

He held out his arms. "Yes, baby, it's me."

She shook her head, suspicion written all over her. "You're not the one who's supposed to come get me."

McBride pushed himself to his feet. Clare took a swift step backward. "No, honey. It's okay. I'm not going to hurt you. I'd never hurt you."

"Mama said you didn't want to take care of me anymore," Clare said, accusation in her voice.

The memory of the dead woman lying in her own blood flashed through his mind. "She didn't know what she was saying, Clare."

"My name's Casey," she said firmly.

"I know. I used to call you that. Casey." He said her nickname the way she said it. "I didn't give you away, Casey. I love you. I'd never give you away. You were taken from me."

"Mama said my real mommy was dead."

"She is, sweetie." He thought of Laura, and ached with the knowledge that she'd gone to her grave without seeing her little girl again. "But I'm alive and I never gave you up."

As he said the words, he felt guilt hit him like a freight

train. He *had* given her up, hadn't he? Five years ago, he'd let her die in his heart and mind. If it hadn't been for Lily, she'd still be dead to him.

If for no other reason, he would love Lily forever for giving his daughter back to him.

She was so beautiful, he thought, looking at his child. She wasn't the cute little three-year-old he'd lost, but a tall, thin girl fast approaching the edge of adolescence. He'd lost six years of her life.

He noticed the ragged stuffed toy she clutched against her chest. Mr. Green had changed, too, he thought with sadness. "I see you still have old Mr. Green. Has he been taking good care of you, marshmallow?"

Her eyes widened and she took a step forward. "Sing the song," she demanded.

He blinked with surprise. The song?

Then he remembered. Laura had made up a lullaby and they had sung it to Clare every night. He closed his eyes and willed the long-buried words to come to mind. Suddenly, he could hear Laura's sweet, clear voice in his ear, giving him the words.

"Sweet Baby Marshmallow, close your bright eyes,
Old Mr. Sunshine has left the night skies,
He's gone to a picnic on the far side of Mars—"

Clare's soft, little-girl voice finished it for him. "But he left Mrs. Moon to watch over the stars."

She scampered down the steps and flung herself at him. He caught her, certain he would die from the feeling of her solid warmth snuggled against his chest.

In his pocket, his cell phone trilled. He felt Casey's

body twitch against him. For a second, he considered shutting it off, but the caller could be Lily. He grabbed it. "McBride."

It was the patrolman he'd positioned outside Lily's house. "Sir, we've been following Ms. Browning since she left her house about twenty minutes ago. She just drove into the woods and parked on a dirt road."

Clare's voice in his ear was soft and slurred. "I told her where to find me, Daddy."

McBride's heart caught.

"Sir, Mr. Walters and another man headed into the woods behind her about three minutes ago. Should we follow?"

As McBride's blood ran cold, Clare suddenly went stiff in his arms. He held her away from him, searching her pale face. She was staring somewhere beyond him, her eyes fixed. Sightless. It reminded him of Lily during one of her visions. A shudder ran through him.

The patrolman's voice buzzed in his ear. "Sir?"

"Follow," he said tersely, disconnecting.

Casey went limp in his arms for a second, then reached out her little hands to clutch at his shirt. "Lily's in trouble!" she cried, a ragged edge of panic to her voice.

"Lily's in trouble?" he repeated, trying to understand.

Then he heard a gunshot.

He caught Clare's chin in his hand, made her look at him. He kept his voice soft, trying not to scare her. "Baby, I need you to do something for me."

LILY HEARD A CRACK behind her, and a whistling sound fly by her ear. Adrenaline exploded inside her, spurring her to greater speed. She had to draw them away from the schoolhouse.

Then she heard something else. "Lily!" It was Casey's voice, as loud as if the child was right beside her. Lily stumbled, almost falling.

"Daddy's here," Casey whispered in her ear. "He says run to the schoolhouse. He'll take care of us."

Lily shook her head. "They want to hurt you."

"He's here! He said to tell you his name is Jubal and he'll take care of us. Hurry!"

His name is Jubal. Lily's heart skipped a beat as hope flooded her, nearly knocking her off her feet.

"Hurry!" Casey's voice began to fade.

Another gunshot shattered the calm of the woods. The tree next to Lily exploded in a shower of wood splinters, peppering her face and arms.

Her heart pounding in her throat, Lily changed course, racing toward the schoolhouse spire barely visible through the pines.

McBride's there with Casey, she chanted with each pounding step. *He'll take care of us.*

MCBRIDE HELD HIS DAUGHTER close, peering out the schoolhouse window. He called in more backup, including Theo Baker. McBride had his gun and a second clip in his pocket—*never leave home without 'em,* he thought with a grim smile—but he couldn't keep Lily safe if she didn't show up.

Two long minutes later, he saw a flurry of movement in the woods. Lily burst through a gap in the trees into the clearing, flying at a full run toward the schoolhouse.

"Stay here," he admonished Clare. He ran out on the

porch. Aiming his gun toward the rustling sounds coming from the woods, he fired two quick shots while Lily took the rickety schoolhouse steps two at a time.

He caught her outstretched hand and pulled her inside, tucking her between him and his daughter. "Are you hurt?"

She shook her head, her golden eyes moving from his face to Clare's and back again. She went pale as a ghost for a second, and he put out a hand to keep her from toppling over.

"You found us!" Clare threw herself at Lily.

Lily's arms tightened around McBride's daughter. She buried her face in the little girl's dark hair. "You're here." She looked up at McBride. "How?"

He spared a second to glance at her. "I believed it was possible."

Her smile spread over him like sunshine, giving him a surge of confidence. He peered out the window, watching for movement. His cover fire had apparently given Lily's pursuers pause.

"I saw the sketch," he told her. "The man you saw in the woods is Joe Britt, Andrew Walters's campaign manager."

"Andrew Walters is with him." Lily's voice darkened. "Abby's own father was in on it."

McBride stared at her in shock and revulsion. He reached for Clare, running his hand over her slim back. She leaned against him, shattering his heart into a million little pieces.

Suddenly, he heard a soft, scraping sound at the back of the schoolhouse. He whirled, peering through the gloom of the darkened room toward the slivers of light at the far end, where the weathered pine had buckled and split over the years, letting in daylight. A dark shadow passed across one of the boards and stopped.

"One of them is back there," McBride murmured. "Cover your ears."

He aimed his weapon at the dark shadow still evident across one of the openings. Taking a deep breath to steady his aim, he fired. A howl of pain answered.

The front steps of the schoolhouse creaked. McBride flattened himself against the wall, his heart racing. He hoped his first shot had taken out the man at the back, because until help arrived, he was outmanned and possibly outgunned.

"Sirens," Clare murmured against his arm.

"Shh, baby," he whispered. Then he heard them. Sirens. At least two cars, probably three, moving in their direction.

The cavalry had finally arrived.

The creaking on the front porch stopped. A second later, McBride heard something crashing through the underbrush. He edged to the doorway in time to catch sight of Andrew Walters running away.

Part of him wanted to pursue, to run Walters down and beat the hell out of him. It was bad enough he'd put his own child in danger for God knew what reason. He'd come here to kill Lily and Clare. McBride had no doubt about it.

But first he had to neutralize Joe Britt as a danger.

"Pull those desks in a circle and hide under them," McBride told Lily. She went right to work, while he slipped outside and crept around the back of the schoolhouse.

He found Joe Britt on the ground, curled up in a ball of agony. His kneecap was a bloody mass of tissue, bone and singed Italian silk. He didn't even try to go for his gun as McBride bent to retrieve it.

He was checking Britt for other weapons when he heard footsteps rapidly approaching. He whirled around, gun trained.

Theo Baker held up his hands. "Whoa, Tex."

McBride lowered his gun. "Finish searching this piece of sh—" He bit back the rest of the curse, aware of his daughter just inside the schoolhouse.

As Theo took over, McBride went around to the front of the schoolhouse. Eight uniformed policemen swarmed the area, two of them holding Andrew Walters by his upper arms. His hands were cuffed behind his back. He met McBride's gaze for a brief second before lowering his head.

Rage boiling in his gut, McBride forced himself to keep his voice calm. "Lily? You and Clare can come out now. It's over."

Lily emerged from the schoolhouse, her arm around Clare's thin shoulders. She met his eyes with a look so full of emotion it made his breath catch. She joined him at the foot of the steps, her gaze moving past him to settle on Andrew Walters.

Before McBride realized what she was going to do, she'd thrust Clare into his grasp and launched herself toward the politician, her small fist connecting with his jaw. The blow was hard enough to snap his head back.

As a couple of officers grabbed her to keep her from landing a second blow, Lily growled, "You heartless son of a bitch! Your own daughter!"

"Nobody was supposed to get hurt," Andrew blurted.

"Have you read him his rights?" McBride asked as the officers holding Lily handed her over to him.

"Yes, sir!" one answered with a grin.

McBride couldn't return the smile. He just gathered Lily and Clare close, thanking God he'd gotten to them both in time.

THE EMERGENCY ROOM DOCTOR assured them Casey was in good health, though he wanted to keep her overnight for observation. But McBride wasn't convinced, hovering by the bed long after the little girl had drifted off to sleep.

Lily had already been debriefed by Theo Baker and now sat in an armchair on the other side of the bed, her fingers still entwined with Casey's. The events of the day had begun to sink in, crushing her beneath the mingled joy and horror.

What was going to happen to Abby? Poor baby, to have lost her mother so horribly, to go through the fear and the abuse she'd suffered at the hands of her kidnappers, only to have her father taken away when she needed him most.

Her body thrumming with exhaustion, Lily almost missed the tingle radiating from her spine. But when the door in her mind swept open, she hurried into the mist, hoping she'd find a pair of blue eyes waiting on the other side. She found herself in a dark room, sitting on the edge of a soft mattress.

Abby sat in the middle of a mound of pillows, her knees tucked up to her chest. Lily touched her. Abby gave a start. "Lily? Did you hear me calling?"

Lily caught her up in her arms. "I'm here."

"I was afraid you'd gone forever," Abby whispered.

"I told you she'd come. She'll always find us."

Lily looked up and met the eyes of McBride's daughter.

Lily stroked Abby's hair, wondering how much her aunt had told her about her father. "Are you okay, Abby?"

"Aunt Jenn says I'll be staying here with her and Uncle David 'cause Mommy's in heaven and Daddy's got to go away for a while." Abby sniffled, her tears warm against Lily's neck. "But Casey promised you'll come see me."

Lily exchanged a glance with Casey, whose solemn little face looked old for its years. "You bet I will." She felt the tug of the mists at her back. Clinging to Abby as her head began to pound, she tried to hold on.

"We have to go, Abby." Casey crossed to Lily and took her hand. "We'll see you again, I promise."

Lily let Casey lead her back through the enveloping mists. When she opened her eyes, she was in the hospital room, her hand still curled around Casey's. The girl's sleepy eyes gazed up at her.

McBride's voice rumbled in her ear. "Where'd you go?"

Lily squeezed Casey's hand. "Abby needed to see us."

McBride's happy expression faltered. "Poor baby. How will her life ever be normal again?"

Lily wasn't sure if he was talking about Abby or his daughter. Maybe it didn't matter. "She's with people who love her enough to get her through it, whatever it takes."

Theo Baker stuck his head in the hospital room

doorway and beckoned for them to join him. Lily gave Casey's hand another squeeze and followed McBride to the door.

Theo lowered his voice. "Britt's telling everything he knows. He wants to make sure Walters doesn't put it all on him. Seems Walters was down double digits in his campaign's internal polls, like Blackledge said. He and Britt got desperate."

And they'd gone for the sympathy vote, using his own daughter. Lily's heart clenched as she thought of Abby.

"Britt hired Gordon and Scotera to carjack Debra Walters. It was supposed to make the papers, garner public sympathy."

"But Debra fought back," McBride guessed.

"Once that happened, Gordy and Skeet went rogue. Walters and Britt didn't know where to find them till they called Lily."

"That's why Andrew Walters wanted me on the case," Lily realized. "They used me to find their missing accomplices."

Theo nodded. "When the kidnappers called you but didn't leave instructions for the ransom drop, Britt figured they were giving Walters a message on how to contact them. They'd had a preplanned meeting place to hand over Abby, so Walters went and left a note for the kidnappers there. When Scotero showed up to check for a message, Britt was there, hiding. He followed Skeet to the trailer."

"And killed them there." McBride's expression turned grim.

"They wanted more money. He decided they were a risk."

"What about when Britt was chasing Abby in the woods?" Lily asked.

"Britt swears he wasn't going to hurt her. He just wanted to find her before she could talk to anyone else, in case Skeet and Gordy had said something to her about what was going on."

"Politics." McBride grimaced. "I hope they nail Britt and Walters to the wall." He looked over his shoulder at his daughter, his expression softening. She'd fallen back to sleep.

Theo put his hand on McBride's shoulder. "I'm glad about Clare. It's a real miracle."

McBride slanted a warm look at Lily. "Yes, it is."

Theo flashed a smile at Lily and left them alone.

McBride walked back to his sleeping daughter's bedside. He touched a wisp of hair curling on her cheek. "You found her, Lily. Just like you said." His voice was thick with emotion.

"No, Casey found me." They'd decided to call her Casey to make her feel more comfortable. Lily had a feeling it would be Clare's name from now on.

A new name for a new and happier life.

Pulling her close, McBride kissed Lily, his touch setting off a thousand little fires up and down her spine. Releasing her mouth, he whispered, "Forgive me for everything I said this morning."

"I understood." She tried to reassure him, but he pressed his fingers to her lips, shushing her.

"No, I need to say this. I realized it didn't matter whether you were right or wrong. You tried to help me. I could never hate you for trying to help me." His lips curved. "I love you too much."

"I love you, too." She touched his cheek. "I can't believe you stumbled onto Casey by accident."

"It wasn't an accident."

She cocked her eyebrow, surprised.

"I think I was supposed to take that exit instead of staying on the interstate. I was supposed to find her."

She shook her head, smiling at the irony. "That's mighty unskeptical of you, Jubal McBride."

He grinned. "I know. I don't think Delaine Howard was a fake, either." He told her about the mailbox he'd found. "The woman who had Clare was named Grainger. Just like the people I told you about, the family with the little girl that Delaine thought was Clare. When I saw the mailbox, I remembered something about those Graingers. The little girl's father had been divorced a few years earlier, after his three-year-old daughter, Gina, died of leukemia. It was one reason we thought he might have Clare, having lost a little girl like that."

"The woman who had Clare was Mr. Grainger's ex-wife."

McBride nodded. "I think so."

"So…what? Mrs. Grainger happened to be walking by and saw Casey playing alone in the yard?"

"I doubt we'll ever know, but I'm going to look into it."

"So you believed Casey was alive all on your own, huh?"

He grinned. "Yeah, I did." He tightened his arms around her. "I saw a miracle today, Lily," he murmured in her ear. "I saw my dead daughter walk out of that schoolhouse alive. I watched that little girl send you a message clear across the woods, and now I'm looking at you both here with me, safe and sound. I'll never scoff at your visions again."

She tilted her head back. "McBride..."

"Marry me, Lily. I can't imagine the rest of my life without you."

She arched an eyebrow. "Is that a question or a command?"

He laughed. "Whichever gets you down the aisle with me."

She chuckled. "Oh, I've had it on good authority for a while that you're the man I'm going to marry. Rose told me so days ago. And I never argue with my sister about such matters."

"Rose told you?" His brow furrowed.

"Did I forget to tell you both of my sisters have special gifts of their own?"

He looked down at her in mock horror.

She laughed. "It appears to run in both our families."

He looked back at Casey. "She does have a gift, doesn't she? Laura always swore her side of the family had 'the sight.'"

Despite his earlier assurances, Lily's stomach tightened as she searched his expression. "Are you okay with that?"

"She saved you with her gift. And you saved her with yours." He claimed her mouth with a deep kiss that drove away the last of Lily's doubts. Her gift—her amazing gift that she'd too long seen as a curse—had brought her more joy and hope than she'd ever imagined possible.

He released her and lifted her face, gazing into her eyes. A smile carved lines into his rugged cheeks. "Thanks for showing me how to believe again."

She wrapped her arms around him and rested her head on his shoulder, looking past him to where his daughter—soon to be hers, too—lay sleeping.

My pleasure, she thought.

1107/46a

CHOOSE:
A QUICK DEATH...
OR A SLOW POISON...

About to be executed for murder, Yelena is offered the chance to become a food taster. She'll eat the best meals, have rooms in the palace – and risk assassination by anyone trying to kill the Commander of Ixia.

But disasters keep mounting as rebels plot to seize Ixia and Yelena develops magical powers she can't control. Her life is threatened again and choices must be made. But this time the outcomes aren't so clear...

Available 21st September 2007

A SEARCH FOR SURVIVORS BECOMES A RACE AGAINST TIME – AND A KILLER

When a plane goes down in the Appalachian mountains, rescue teams start looking for the survivors and discover that a five-year-old boy and a woman are missing. Twenty miles from the crash site, Deborah Sanborn has a vision of two survivors, and she senses these strangers are in terrible danger.

With the snow coming down, not only are they racing against time and the elements – they're up against a killer desperate to silence his only living witness to murder.

Available 21st September 2007

FREE

4 BOOKS AND A SURPRISE GIFT!

We would like to take this opportunity to thank you for reading this Mills & Boon® book by offering you the chance to take FOUR more specially selected titles from the Intrigue series absolutely FREE! We're also making this offer to introduce you to the benefits of the Mills & Boon® Reader Service™—

- ★ **FREE home delivery**
- ★ **FREE gifts and competitions**
- ★ **FREE monthly Newsletter**
- ★ **Books available before they're in the shops**
- ★ **Exclusive Reader Service offers**

Accepting these FREE books and gift places you under no obligation to buy; you may cancel at any time, even after receiving your free shipment. Simply complete your details below and return the entire page to the address below. You don't even need a stamp!

YES! Please send me 4 free Intrigue books and a surprise gift. I understand that unless you hear from me, I will receive 6 superb new titles every month for just £3.10 each, postage and packing free. I am under no obligation to purchase any books and may cancel my subscription at any time. The free books and gift will be mine to keep in any case.

I7ZEE

Ms/Mrs/Miss/Mr...Initials ....
BLOCK CAPITALS PLEASE

Surname ....

Address ....

....

....Postcode ....

Send this whole page to:

The Reader Service, FREEPOST CN81, Croydon, CR9 3WZ